MESS WITH ME

KYLIE GILMORE

Cover design by Sweet 'N Spicy Designs

Published by: Extra Fancy Books

ISBN-13: 978-1-942238-34-8

Because a romance book club would rock…

1

—————

Ally Bloom stepped into her college reunion, looking for her lost love and prepared for rapture.

Where the heck is he? She scanned the huge ballroom of the hotel for her target, coming up empty. Lots of twentysomethings pushing thirty mingled in cocktail dresses and suits, chatting about the "old" days four years ago back at UConn (University of Connecticut).

Show yourself, man of my dreams. She and Dean had been texting back and forth over the past month and, after he'd said he couldn't wait to see her at the reunion, his texts had become increasingly flirty, calling her beautiful and gorgeous. *Bring your dancing shoes, gorgeous.* It felt like a lead-in to a fresh start.

She casually skirted the edges of the dance floor, hoping to sense the presence of her tall, dark, and handsome man for a passionate rekindling of love. The attraction would pull them together as inevitably as two moths to a flame but with less incendiary results.

Not finding him, she wandered over to the bar, ordered the special, a fruity punch spiked with vodka, and took a sip. Should she work the room, wait for the dinner buffet and hopefully spot him at a table, or maybe ask the DJ to play her and Dean's song? But what if Dean didn't remember their song? They'd only danced to it once at his frat's formal senior year.

Maybe I'll text him. No, wait. She wanted the *wow* factor of a face-to-face meeting considering the time she'd put in prepping for this event—hair, makeup, killer strapless red dress with matching pumps. Not to mention she'd gotten waxed, legs only because she could *not* take anything more intimately painful. Been there, smacked the esthetician. But these were the sacrifices she made to offer herself at her personal height of feminine beauty and appeal. Their love would do the rest.

She hoped.

Where was he?

She watched the doorway, where people were still arriving. Maybe he'd step through the archway of navy blue, white, and gray balloons, their eyes would meet across the room and they'd communicate in that single loving gaze that there was nothing more they ever needed than each other.

She sighed and took a healthy swallow of spiked punch. It had been so long since she'd been interested in any man. Some part of her wondered if it was because she was meant to be with Dean. And when her class organized a reunion so soon—normally it was five or ten years for classes to get back together—it felt like another sign from the universe. Fate had plans for them and it would be foolish not to be open to the possibility of a reconnection. Dean was her first love; they'd met sophomore year in a computer science 101 course that they were both completely lost in. They'd dated until a year after graduation when Dean declared he was "too young to settle down."

She'd floundered.

Four months later in a total rebound situation, she'd briefly fallen for Mark, gotten engaged, and fled her own wedding, leaving poor Mark at the altar. At the time, she'd realized she was still in love with Dean. She'd called Dean immediately after—still in her wedding gown, for crying out loud—only to discover he had a girlfriend.

She blew out a breath that made her blond bangs lift off her forehead. The anticipation was killing her.

A tall man with short dirty blond hair across the room caught her eye. He stood, arms crossed in a white button-down shirt and black pants (no suit jacket or tie), taking in the room, his face set in a hard expression. Oh, hey, was that Ethan Case? He was one of the guys that grew up with the Campbell brothers. She'd seen him a bunch of times at Garner's bar, hanging with the guys, but had never really talked to him one-on-one. She lifted a hand in a small wave that he missed because he turned and said something to the woman at his side, a tall brunette with a short cap of hair, in a black dress. Oh, it was his girlfriend, Cali. You could tell how close they were by the way they spoke in such a close intimate manner. Though neither of them smiled or touched each other. Well, not everyone was as affectionate as she and Dean were.

"Ally?" a familiar masculine voice asked.

She turned and gasped at the sudden appearance of Dean, which somehow made her choke on her own spit. She coughed like crazy and the love of her life helpfully pounded her on the back.

"You okay?" he asked with a laugh. "Didn't mean to sneak up on you like that."

"I'm fine," she gasped out, her eyes watering. "Hi." She coughed some more.

He smiled his dimpled smile. "Breathe."

She did. "Yeah." She sipped her punch, trying to regain the composure needed for their rapturous reunion.

Dean pulled her in for a quick hug. "So good to see you again. How you been?"

"Great!" She studied his handsome features, a little startled by his new look. They hadn't texted current pics of each other. The man she remembered was a lacrosse jock who loved his frat, with shaggy dark brown hair and a scruffy jaw. Now his hair was short and neat, his jaw clean-shaven except for a small patch of hair on his chin. What was that called? A soul patch? The silver hoop earring was also new.

He smiled, his brown eyes warm on hers. "Feels like old times being back for Homecoming weekend, seeing you. Did you catch the game?"

She'd missed the football game due to her massive preparations for this moment. "Nope. Just made it here. So how's Wall Street treating you?"

He rocked back and forth on the balls of his feet. "Actually, being a stockbroker wasn't for me. I'm selling solar panels now."

She tensed. When she'd asked him by text earlier about the world of stocks, he'd said *living the dream!* Clearly, he'd forgotten he'd said that. The lie rankled. *Regroup.* A fresh start meant things would be different, but that didn't mean he wasn't the same affectionate loving man underneath.

She smiled, leaning closer and looking up at him under her lashes. "I'm so happy for you."

"Thanks." He gave her a blatant once-over. "Damn, you're smoking in that dress." His hands went to her waist, spiking her body temperature. His voice was husky by her ear. "I got a room upstairs. Why don't we head up?"

She jerked away. "Wh-what?"

He moved closer and admired her cleavage. "For old times' sake."

She frowned, her heart sinking somewhere in the vicinity of her perfectly smooth ankles. "You said to bring my dancing shoes—"

"We'll be dancing all right. The horizontal monkey dance." He waggled his eyebrows. "In the sheets," he added as if she might've missed his sleazy reference.

"I thought—" she nearly choked on her anger, on the complete mismatch of their expectations "—I thought you were remembering how good we were together. I thought this was a fresh start."

"Ally." His condescending tone cut deep. "You know I love you, but I don't *love* you. Understand? I'm not into you in *that way*. I just thought we could have a little fun."

The breath knocked right out of her. Not *that way*? She

sucked in air, her heart thundering in her ears, her hands icy. She struggled to comprehend. They'd been together for four years, madly in love. "How could it not be *that way*?"

He gave her a sympathetic look that twisted the knife in her gut. "Things changed." He waved at someone over her shoulder. "Olivia!" He turned back to her with a warm smile. "Great to see you, Ally. Take care."

Then he left, heading over to Olivia, a gorgeous woman in a tight pale lavender dress with black fuck-me stilettos.

She stood there for a full minute in total shock, shaky and cold, so very cold. How many women had he texted to reconnect with at this event? Her gut churned.

His laugh reached her, where he was holding Olivia's hand, walking out with her. Probably to go to his room for a "little fun."

She couldn't bear it. She did an about-face, walked out of the ballroom, down the hallway, and straight to the ladies' room.

Unfortunately, there was a line out the door. Dammit, could this night get any worse?

She headed across the hall to the empty men's room and hid inside a stall. Why had she built this up in her mind? This wasn't *fate*. This was total BS. Her fury both at herself for her ridiculously high hopes and him for being such a *guy* quickly morphed to tears. She gave in to a good cry, still holding her spiked punch, and carefully not touching the toilet.

Promise me you'll think things through before jumping into another relationship. Her mom's voice in her head just made her cry harder. After her almost wedding to Mark, Ally had promised her mom she'd be less impulsive. Like mother, like daughter. Her mom had been impulsive, jumping in with both feet with the wrong man, and ended up single and pregnant with Ally's oldest sister, Serena. Things had worked out for her mom eventually with Ally's dad, who loved Serena like his own daughter, but it could've been a much more difficult situation. One that easily could've happened to Ally as well. Not meant to be—not then and not now.

She tried to get a full breath and ended up with a hiccupping gasp, the tears still flowing. Her love life could not be more sucky. All this time she'd told herself she'd avoid the heartache her mom had endured by finding the perfect prince for her happy-ever-after. That blind faith in a happy ending had brought her to this moment, forgiving and forgetting with Dean, allowing him into her heart a second time. She had to stop living in this romantic fantasy world, impulsively jumping in, heart on her sleeve. It didn't help her avoid the pain of heartbreak. If anything, it made things a thousand times worse. Real life didn't work that way.

Believing in the fairy tale was a dead end.

The truth of that hit her like a slap. She took a deep shuddering breath and wiped the tears from her cheeks.

I need a new direction. The quiet certainty of her inner voice gave her a brief moment of calm.

Someone came in. Shit. Hopefully they wouldn't notice her. Of course, if they looked under the stall, they might see her cute red pumps. She held her breath as the guy did his business and then washed his hands. That was nice. She appreciated a guy who washed his hands; they didn't all do that. Her ex-fiancé hadn't. Dean did. A small sob escaped.

Shiny black shoes approached her stall. He knocked.

She froze, not even breathing.

"Do you need some assistance, ma'am?" he asked in a voice that sounded vaguely familiar and cop-like.

Her voice came out small. "No, I'm okay."

"Are you aware you're in the men's room?"

She laughed and then choked on a sob. "Yes. The ladies' room had a line." She dashed at her eyes, but the tears were back with a vengeance. So much buildup for this reunion of lost love and all she got was a good cry in the men's room with a witness to her humiliation.

"Are you crying, ma'am? Has someone hurt you? I'm a police officer. I can help."

She knew he sounded cop-like. She peeked through the crack next to the door. Ethan Case, looking tough and capable and concerned.

She opened the door and stepped out. "Hi, Ethan."

"Ally!" He took in her no doubt ruined makeup, her tearstained face (she was not a pretty crier), and the drink she still held in her hand. "What happened?"

She was way beyond social niceties at this distress level and told him exactly what was wrong. "The usual, complete and utter annihilation of the heart." She tossed back her punch, crumpled the plastic cup and tossed it in the garbage.

Ethan held the men's room door open for her, still looking concerned. She stepped out to the hallway and then leaned against the wall. He stood in front of her, his hard blue eyes scanning her features. Probably looking for signs of a physical altercation.

She waved him on. "I just need some time to pull it together. You go ahead back to your date."

"Are you going to cry some more?" he asked gruffly.

"Probably."

"You, uh, want to talk about it?"

Her eyes widened, surprised that he'd offered. It wasn't like they knew each other that well. Of course, he did have an honorary little sister, her friend Mad Campbell. Maybe he was used to female drama. Still, she had more tears in her and would prefer not to have a witness to her breakdown. Her fantasy happy-ever-after was dead and she needed time to mourn. "No, thank you."

"Okay." He hesitated, staring at her for a long moment before walking away, looking back at her several times and then disappearing back into the ballroom.

She walked in the opposite direction, turned the corner to an empty hallway and took a seat on the floor. Who cared if her dress got wrinkled? Nobody, that was who. She bent her knees, wrapping her arms around them, and rested her head on top. She felt like a complete fool the way she'd built up Dean and what they'd had in her mind. Those four years together meant nothing to him. How could he love her and *not* love her? His utter indifference compared to her dream of a loving reunion brought fresh tears. She let them fall, the world going blurry. All of her three older sisters were married. Her friends were all finding their forever loves and she had nobody. Maybe she never would. Without the rosy belief in a fairy-tale love, what would her life be like? Alone, probably, no one to hold her but herself. It sucked, but guess what? So did her love life, so which was worse?

Finally, she finished crying and wiped her eyes with a tissue from her purse. She stood and took a deep breath, contemplating if she should bail on the reunion or go back in and prove she was just as over Dean as he was over her. He'd probably be back inside of ten minutes, she thought uncharitably. He hadn't been all that in the bedroom.

Her pride had her taking a step back to the reunion. She halted in surprise.

Ethan was standing at the end of the hallway, where she'd just spent the last several minutes crying her eyes out. Had he seen?

She crossed to him. "What're you doing here?"

"Same as you. Taking a breather. Come on, they're serving dinner. You can sit with me and Cali."

Suddenly there was nothing she'd rather do. Ethan was a connection to her friends, a comforting oasis in this treacherous territory. "Okay, thanks."

They walked in silence for a few moments before Ethan said in a mock growl, "Say the word and I'll give the guy who made you cry a fat lip."

She let out a shaky laugh. "Thanks."

"Men suck," he said and ruffled her hair.

She didn't even care that he'd mussed it. "They do."

"Being single's not so bad," he said gently.

Easy for him to say, he had a girlfriend. "What're you doing here anyway? I mean, the reunion. I know you weren't at UConn when I was here. You're too old."

He bumped her with his hip. "Take that back, young'un."

She laughed. "You're thirtysomething, right?"

"Yeah. Cali went here."

She searched her memory and came up short. "Huh. Guess we didn't have any classes together."

One corner of his mouth lifted. "You'll get along with her great. She thinks men suck too."

"Even you?"

He cracked a rare smile that lit up his face in an astonishingly gorgeous flash. "I'm the exception."

2

———

Ethan hadn't been paying attention where Ally was concerned. Even with cry face, she was strikingly beautiful in a sexy pixie way. Blond shoulder-length hair with bangs that bounced in time with her energetic movements, guileless wide blue eyes, cute straight nose, a sweet bow in her top lip, lusciously plump bottom lip, petite yet busting with curves in a tight red dress. How was it he'd never spent time with her? She was one of Mad Campbell's friends from that women's book club. He'd definitely seen Ally around, usually elbow deep in women. Now his eyes were open. That she was showing signs of cheering up because of his small efforts made him feel like a hero.

They entered the large ballroom of the reunion and he found his date, Cali, standing stiffly, legs apart in a ready stance, scanning the room with narrowed eyes. Even off duty she was always on. She was his partner, a great cop with a long-term plan to become police chief. He was her date tonight as a buffer against her former classmates, three asshole guys in particular from her criminal justice classes who'd made it their mission to make Cali feel like an inter-loper, calling her "weak geek" and a "guy wannabe" every chance they got. He knew her only as a tough competent cop. They frequently stepped in for each other on social occasions, but never once considered seeing each other. She was focused on her career. He refused to date a coworker. Besides, he preferred more softness in a woman, probably to make up for what he lacked in his own life.

"Hey," he said, stopping in front of Cali with Ally.

Cali snapped to attention. "Where were you?" she asked through clenched teeth. "You're supposed to be my plus one." She stared at Ally. "Who are you?"

Ethan made the introductions. Then he spoke directly to Cali under his breath. "She's having a rough night, so dial it back."

Ally smiled at Cali. "Nice to meet you up close. I saw you with Ethan from afar once at Garner's."

"You too," Cali said, still sounding pissed.

"She's sitting with us for dinner," Ethan told Cali.

"Fine," Cali replied, her eyes darting around the room. "Just don't leave me alone like that again." She gave him a fierce glare. "I looked like a loser standing here by myself."

"Why didn't you go talk to someone?" Ethan asked, which dialed the glare to death-ray level.

Cali whispered fiercely in his ear, "Two of my enemies aren't here and the other flat out ignored my hello. Looked right at me and turned his head away."

He nodded once, his jaw tight. "Sorry." He was pissed on her behalf at the slight and also pissed he hadn't been at her side for it. Together they would've taken that guy down so fast. Metaphorically speaking. But he hadn't wanted to leave Ally all alone in her distress.

Cali lifted her chin, stoic in the face of adversity.

"I love your dress," Ally told Cali. "Where'd you get it?"

Cali looked down at herself. "Thanks. My mom got it for me for college graduation years ago. I have no idea where it came from."

"Well, it's super cute," Ally said.

"Should we eat?" Cali asked.

Ally nodded. "I could eat."

"Let's go." He crooked his elbow, offering his arm to Cali to soothe her ruffled feathers. She gripped his shirt over his bicep and he shifted her hand to rest on his forearm. She wasn't great with social stuff. He understood her because his "little sister" Mad was the same way—one of the guys and not quite up to speed on the whole woman-man flirting thing. Ally walked on his other side. He considered offering his arm to her too, but decided against it. One woman on his arm was plenty.

After they piled their plates with an assortment of prime rib, lemon chicken, and pasta, they settled at a table. Some people joined them and introduced themselves. Ally knew a couple of them. No one seemed to remember Cali or the other way around. It had been that way all night.

"You sure you went here?" he whispered to Cali.

"I spent a lot of time studying in the library," Cali responded in a low voice. "Or at the gym."

Figured. She had a master's degree in criminal justice and was sculpted muscle from head to toe.

Cali was quiet, staring at her plate. "I shouldn't have come," she mumbled. "It was a stupid idea."

Oh fuck. He'd never seen her upset. He elbowed her. "Hey, we can still have fun. We'll show off our moves on the dance floor."

She snorted. "I don't dance."

"We'll slow dance, okay? It'll be good."

Cali lifted watery eyes to his. "Thank you."

A twinge of sympathy made his chest ache. He was no softie, but seeing the tough Cali near tears got to him. Maybe because he was also stoic and tough. "No problem." He checked in with Ally on his other side, who was attacking a pile of baked ziti with gusto. "Feeling a little better?"

"Actually, yeah. Comfort food helps." She smiled at him and Cali. "Plus knowing I'm with friends."

He warmed to be counted as a friend after such a short time. He must've done something right to make her feel comfortable with him and cheer up a bit. Women tended to flirt with him, not consider him a friend.

Dinner was quiet at their end of the table. Cali and Ally finished eating and became very subdued. Neither of them wanted dessert. The music started up again, some loud club music, the DJ hollering at them to get out there and dance.

Cali stood abruptly, so he stood too. "Let's go," she said. "I don't need to prove anything to anyone."

He understood. She was quick to cut her losses. Still, what about Ally?

"You want to stop for coffee?" he asked Cali, figuring he could invite Ally along too. He and Cali frequently had coffee after a rough shift at work. The simple act of drinking a cup of joe helped them come back to the realm of normality. Some of the stuff they saw on the job stuck with them and not in a good way.

"Perfect," Cali replied.

He leaned down to where Ally sat, speaking close to her ear so she could hear him over the loud music. She smelled like flowers, delicate and soft. "We're heading out, stopping for coffee, if you want to come along."

Ally looked from him to Cali. "I wouldn't want to intrude."

"Let's go," Cali said and strode to the exit.

"It's not a problem," Ethan told Ally.

"Sure?" Ally asked.

Cali was already halfway to the door.

"Yeah, I'm sure," he said.

Ally took one last look around, her gaze stopping on a dark-haired man with a soul patch standing with a group of guys, all of them yukking it up like they were back at the frat. She turned back to Ethan, lifting her chin. "I'd love to go for coffee."

"Come on, we gotta move it. Cali's probably in the car with the engine running by now."

She laughed and they headed out, walking at a brisk pace. He quickly gave her directions to a diner nearby and headed for Cali's old Chevy, which was in fact running, Cali staring straight ahead in the driver's seat.

A short while later, they were seated in a quiet booth in the back of the diner. He sat on the bench seat next to Cali, who seemed more relaxed now, though still subdued. Across the table, Ally rested her head in her hand and sighed. For the first time ever, he was the only cheerful guy with a bunch of sad sacks. Hmm…what to do. Before he could come up with anything, Ally spoke up.

"I really appreciate you guys letting me tag along. I came here tonight for one specific purpose and it was a complete disaster."

"What was it?" Cali asked, surprising him. She was usually quiet during their de-stress cup of joe.

Ally glanced at him.

"Doesn't leave this room," he assured her.

Cali nodded.

Ally took a deep breath and then in a flood of words told them all about Dean Sweeney (rhymes with weenie), her first love in a serious four-year-long relationship, and how much she'd hoped tonight would be their rapturous reunion of lost love.

He sat there in stunned silence at the raw confession. This was a woman who loved in a big way. Cali was silent too.

Ally didn't need any encouragement. She kept going, speaking in her animated way, hands gesturing, blond bangs bouncing in time with her movements. She told them how, after she and Dean broke up, she had hot sex with Mark based on some erotic romance novel, and she thought that meant he was the One, so she quickly got engaged to him, and then ran away at the altar because of Dean, who had a girlfriend. His head was spinning, but he was pretty sure he was following as she barreled on, confessing that she hadn't had sex in way too long, but she'd given up the fantasy and would probably be alone for the rest of her life.

He blinked.

Ally's chin quivered.

His gut clenched. He didn't know how to fix it. He wasn't even sure exactly what she meant. What fantasy? Did sex have something to do with it? Why did she have to be alone if her ex had already moved on?

Cali spoke up. "So that's your problem? Your ex has a girlfriend?"

Ally looked to the ceiling, blinking rapidly in a futile attempt to hold back tears.

He shot Cali a dark look for making Ally cry and then turned to Ally. "You don't have to tell us."

"No, it's okay." Ally sniffled and swiped under her eyes with her finger. Cali grabbed a napkin from the dispenser on the table and tossed it at Ally. "Thanks." She dried her tears with the napkin and took a shaky breath. "He doesn't have a girlfriend now. He said he loves me, but he doesn't love me. Not in *that way*."

"What do you mean not in that way?" Cali asked. Which was his question. What the hell did that even mean? The man spoke in riddles.

"I guess it just means he's not into me anymore," Ally choked out. "Unless I want to hook up for old times' sake."

"Bastard," he spat.

Cali scowled. "He needs to be neutered."

Ally burst out laughing. "He does." She quickly dropped her smile, clearly still hurting.

The waitress arrived to take their orders. Ally gave the waitress a tight smile and ordered a coffee with extra cream and sugar, even adding a please at the end. Down in the dumps and heartbroken, she still made the effort to speak kindly to their waitress. He liked that kind of internal strength, respected it.

After the waitress left, Ally gave him and Cali a small smile. "I'm sorry I overshared. I'm sure you didn't need to hear the nitty-gritty of my sucky love life."

"No problem," he and Cali said in near unison.

Ally smiled. "You guys are too cute."

She thought he and Cali were a couple. Before he could correct that assumption, Cali piped up.

"My turn to share. I came here tonight with one mission—show my enemies I'm no longer a weak geek and no chance in hell I can be mistaken for a guy wannabe. My weapon of choice—sexy dress that shows off my strong body and a hot date."

Ethan jolted at the hot-date part. "Thanks." Cali never complimented him.

Cali ignored him, instead speaking directly to Ally. "My mission also failed. Two of the guys weren't even there and the other ignored me. I dunno, maybe he didn't recognize me. My hair is shorter now and I had Lasik to correct my vision, so no more thick glasses, but still, I don't think I look that different." She paused, staring off in the distance. "I don't know why it mattered so much to me to show those guys up, but..." She blew out a breath. "My point is, we are simpatico and I feel you, girl."

"Oh, Cali!" Ally exclaimed, brightening instantly. "Thank you for sharing that. I feel so much better knowing I'm not the only one who built up this reunion into some big life-changing deal."

"You are not alone," Cali said.

Ally's face crumpled and then she nodded, her eyes watery, lips pressed together tightly.

Ethan glared at Cali for upsetting Ally again. Cali lifted one shoulder and shot him a look like *not my fault she's a wimp*. He jerked his head toward Ally like *fix it*.

Cali stared at Ally. "Let me guess, your fantasy was a man to sweep you off your feet and bring you everlasting happiness, and now that you've given it up, you're afraid to be just you."

Ally pushed her bangs out of her eyes and whispered, "How did you know?"

Ethan turned to Cali, very interested in her answer. How *did* she know that?

Cali shrugged. "Culture."

That was vague, but Ally seemed satisfied, nodding in agreement. "Too many romantic movies and books from too young an age. I totally bought into the romantic fantasy."

"I depend on no man for my well-being," Cali replied.

"But doesn't Ethan make you happy?" Ally asked.

"*I* make me happy," Cali said bluntly.

The waitress arrived with their coffees. After everyone

had doctored their coffees with cream and sugar, Ally said longingly to Cali, "I *so* want to be you."

Cali blushed, and Ethan bit back a smile. Cali never blushed.

Ally met his eyes, a flash of longing in them, and quickly lowered them, taking a sip of her coffee. Maybe Ally was wishing she was Cali to be with him. Or maybe she just wanted Cali's kick-ass attitude. He wasn't sure and didn't want to show his hand yet. Despite Ally's current distress, his senses were on full alert, completely tuned in to her—blood rushing through his veins, pulse quickened, nerves tingling in his fingers aching to touch. And not just because she was beautiful and sexy as all hell in that dress. His head and heart were in a different place since his foster mom, Peggy, died three weeks ago. It was a wake-up call, losing her, the only mom he'd ever known. He'd never told her he loved her, had never said it to anyone. And now it was too late.

He had no memory of his parents or the car accident that killed them. He'd been three years old, asleep in the backseat. No kin had come forward; his grandparents hadn't wanted to raise a kid again. He'd had no one, bouncing through foster homes until he was eight years old and landed in Peggy's house. Shortly after that, she introduced him to the Campbell family. They made all the difference—Peggy, along with his honorary dad and brothers and sister—but it wasn't blood. He wanted that now more than ever. A family of his own. He was ready, knew he had to be more open because—

He wanted love.

No one had ever said they loved him. Not Peggy, not any of the Campbells, not a girlfriend. Okay, sure, Joe Campbell, his honorary dad, had included him in stuff like that—love you guys, love you knuckleheads—but it had never been specific to *him*. No one had ever said, "I love you, Ethan."

Ally's blond hair fell in her face as she held her mug, staring down at it. He wanted to brush her hair behind her ear, stroke her cheek to see if it was as soft as it looked. Timing was bad. She was too upset. He knew he had to wait, though every instinct was telling him to go for it.

Maybe he'd already been heading in this settled-down direction before Peggy's death. He hadn't taken a woman to his bed in a while. He'd been choosy because he wanted to wake up with someone who made him smile. Maybe that was corny or unrealistic—he wasn't much of a smiler anyway—but that was where he'd drawn the line. He had enough harsh in his line of work and he longed for the simple genuine happiness of waking up to a woman who could make him smile.

Ally looked up and slapped her palm on the table. "Do you have any idea how much time and energy I've wasted looking for love, trying to hang onto love, and hoping for love?"

It seemed like a rhetorical question, so he remained quiet.

"A lot?" Cali guessed.

"Too damn much!" Ally exclaimed. "I was sold a bill of goods that love would solve everything. It doesn't." She slowly shook her head. "I need to learn a new way. I've put my life on hold, waiting for the fairy tale. I need to break free of that mindset." Her blue eyes lit up. "Like a butterfly breaking out of its chrysalis, you know? I need to focus on me and find what will make me happy."

"And what's that?" Ethan asked.

Ally folded her hands on the table and stared at them. "I don't know, but I know I need to find out." She turned to Cali. "I really liked what you said about being responsible for your own happiness."

Cali gave her a high five and Ally turned to him. He gave her one, happy to see her looking more steady and confident.

Ally blew out a breath. "You know, I think maybe subconsciously I was preparing for a solo life. I just moved into a one-bedroom apartment, living alone for the first time in my life, though I did move near friends." She pursed her sexy lips. "And I probably wouldn't have moved if my roommate, Carrie, hadn't moved in with her fiancé." She waved that away. "It still counts." She stared at Cali's sculpted arm. "Maybe I can start with a fitness regimen to take better care of myself. Not even to look good for a guy, just for me." She pulled her phone from her purse. "I'm going to text Charlotte right now. She's a personal trainer. I'll get a session in with her or at least some advice on what to do." She texted rapidly and then put her phone away. "Done."

"You look fit to me," Ethan said casually. *Just pointing out a fact, not lusting over your sexy little body.*

"I'm naturally petite, but I'm not strong." Ally flexed her biceps, which were nonexistent. "I want to be strong like you, Cali."

Cali popped a bicep. "I lift weights."

"That's an idea too." Ally blew out a breath that made her bangs lift. "God, I've lost so much time, so much wasted—" She stopped herself. "I'll make a plan. You know, stuff I want to try. Self-improvement things to kind of meet the new me."

"I like it," Cali said. "The butterfly version of you."

"Yes," Ally breathed. "Yes, I love that."

"Sounds good to me," Ethan put in.

"I'm actually looking forward to it," Ally said firmly with a bob of her head. "A new direction. I'm going to learn to enjoy being single so I can be responsible for my own happiness." Her blue eyes were shining, her smile bright, and he wanted her. In his bed and in his life.

Her new quest to enjoy singlehood should've been a deterrent for him, but it wasn't. Tell him he couldn't do something and he instantly wanted to. Part of his contrary nature that got him where he was today. He'd had a real problem with authority as a kid, angry and belligerent, big chip on his shoulder over no one wanting to adopt him. Not even Peggy, though he'd lived with her the longest. So what did he do? He became the authority figure he once despised. He was careful not to be an ass about it; he was one of the good guys.

Ally sipped her coffee and then put her mug down. "Isn't it funny I came to this conclusion here with you guys? Normally I'd be a little secretly jealous, but no. I'm just happy for you and for me."

Cali's brows scrunched down in puzzlement. Ethan sipped his coffee and said nothing. He had to pick his moment. This wasn't it.

Ally smiled to herself, shaking her head, and then pointed at him. "Isn't it hilarious everyone used to think you were a sex addict when you're so obviously not?" She gestured to Cali, who missed it because she was busy frowning and adjusting her strapless bra. He'd heard all about the evils of underwire on the drive over here.

"Yeah, hilarious," he said deadpan. That had been a rumor started by his honorary dad, Joe, with good intentions to make sure Lauren shifted her focus away from Ethan and onto Alex. Lauren and Alex were now engaged. Ethan didn't take it personally. All for a good cause and he'd lost nothing from Lauren and her friends avoiding him for a few weeks. Besides, it gave him a primo opportunity to play a prank back on Joe. He told him he wouldn't know when it was coming, but it would. Vague threats worked best. Except Joe was a tough cop, Ethan's role model, really, and merely got a good laugh over the threat.

Ally cocked her head at him. "You don't laugh much, do you?"

"No, he doesn't," Cali answered for him, finally done adjusting her boobs. "Neither do I. Life isn't a ha-ha-whee-e-e ride." Her voice rose on the whee-e-e-e in a dry approximation of a good time.

He and Ally took one look at each other and cracked up. Cali remained stoic.

"You should smile more," Ally told him. "It makes you look so much younger and approachable."

Implied insult—smile more, old man. "How do I normally look?" he asked through his teeth.

"Like a tough guy." She hid a smile by sipping her coffee.

"An old tough guy?" he pressed.

"Oops!" Ally said brightly. "Didn't mean to offend. Not old, but what's the word I'm looking for, Cali?"

"Competent," Cali said.

"No-o-o, not that," Ally said.

"Gee, thanks." He lifted his mug, took a sip and nearly spewed coffee with Ally's further explanation.

"What's the word for been around the block a time or

two?" Ally gestured wildly. "You know, the kind of tough guy with no patience for any BS."

"A cop," Cali supplied.

"No-o-o, not that," Ally said.

"Moving on," he grumbled.

Ally pointed at him. "Jaded! You don't smile so much as smirk. I don't think I've ever heard you laugh before today."

"I would if something was ha-ha-whee-e-e-e funny." He grinned.

Ally smiled back. "Keep it up, tough guy, I might think you have a real sense of humor."

He slapped a hand to his chest and staggered a bit in his seat. "Ooh! She wounds me."

Cali piped up. "His favorite joke is brain sucker and it's starving." She put her hand on his head and moved it up and down in imitation of a brain sucker.

"Ha-ha." He fixed his hair. It was short with some spikes in front that looked stupid when they weren't lined up just right.

"That's a classic," Ally said.

"What's your favorite joke?" he asked.

Cali pulled out her phone and started checking it. She wasn't much for joking around. Good. Now he had Ally all to himself.

"Knock, knock," Ally said.

"No," he said.

She smiled sunnily. "You have to answer the door."

"Nobody's home."

"Stopwatch."

He groaned.

"Come on, give it to me," she said.

He smirked, his mind going to its usual dirty place. She gestured for him to hurry up and do his part. "Stopwatch who?" he drawled.

"Stopwatch you're doing and let me in!" She waited, but he couldn't even fake a laugh. Didn't stop her. "What do you call cheese that's not yours?"

He shook his head. "No idea."

She flashed a smile. "That's nach-o cheese. Get it? Not yo, nach-o."

"Stop. Just stop."

She grinned and took a sip of coffee. "I teach first grade, so I could go all night."

He smirked. All night would be awesome.

"There's that smirk again," she said. "What is that about?"

He studied her expression. She looked curious and open, not the kind to judge, so he gave her the truth. "Usually it means I'm refraining from saying the dirty thing that comes to mind. I try to keep the locker room talk to the locker room."

"Why? If it's funny, share it."

"You said you could go all night. Obvious innuendo."

She inclined her head. "None intended, but I see where your mind's at." She looked to Cali, who was still messing with her phone. "Boy, you're awfully busy over there."

Cali didn't bother to look up. "I've got vacation time coming up and need to confirm a few details."

Ally seemed considerably more cheerful than when they first got here. "You feeling better about that loser now?" he asked.

She stopped smiling, her lips pressed into a flat line.

Shut up, genius. She was fine until you brought it up again. "Sorry," he quickly said. "Forget it."

Cali put her phone away. "Just ignore Ethan's smirks. Guys have sex on the brain. It's a flaw of their species."

"Hey," Ethan protested, "that's not true. I've got some important stuff rattling around up there."

"Like what?" Cali asked.

Ally giggled, looking back and forth between Cali and him.

"Like the score of the Sox game," he returned.

Cali put her palm on his face and shoved before turning to Ally. "I wish you the best in your new single lifestyle. You'd be surprised how far you can go when you really focus on your own life."

"Single me, happy me," Ally said in a voice of forceful

determination. "My new motto. A new way of life." She fist-bumped Cali and then raised her fist to him.

He grabbed her fist and held it for a moment. She raised wide blue eyes to his and he released her. Pink crept up her cheeks.

He smiled.

3

Ally's first single me, happy me day was one of those glorious fall days in Connecticut—a sunny comfortable seventy degrees with a light breeze—made even more glorious by her first inspiring Pilates session under her friend Charlotte's direction. Fresh from her workout, she drove straight to the sporting goods store for all the things Charlotte recommended and was now the proud owner of a giant inflatable ball, mat, dumbbell hand weights, and a fitness wristband that promised to report her daily number of steps. Goal—10,000 steps a day. She hit the accelerator, eager to get home for a shower and then get some steps in. It was late Sunday morning, so she had the whole day to activate her new fit lifestyle. Preferably outdoors. Fall was her favorite season and she mentally added "spend more time in nature" to her goal list.

Charlotte's advice to take it "one step at a time" and to "celebrate each small victory" had made the whole process of transformation seem manageable. Of course, she'd meant that in terms of fitness, but Ally took it to heart. She'd be open to new experiences and celebrate positive improvement. Eventually she'd get to a truly happy single butterfly state and that would be a beautiful thing. True contentment—

A police siren went off. Dammit! She checked her

rearview mirror, lights flashing right behind her. Not another ticket. She was still paying the points on her insurance for the last one. And the one before that. The police cruiser pulled in tight behind her car. She pulled over, annoyed at the inconvenience that was harshing her newfound mellow.

The officer made his arrogant swaggering way over to her. Didn't he have anything better to do than pull over innocent citizens going just a teensy bit over the speed limit?

The man peered through the window at her. Ethan! A friendly cop!

She powered down the window and beamed at him. He didn't return her smile, his hard blue eyes drilling into her. He looked even tougher in uniform—all business, no BS. "Hi, Ethan! I just got back from the most amazing workout and shopping for fitness stuff. All part of the single me, happy me plan." At his silence, she added, "How're you?"

"You know why I pulled you over?" he asked with no trace of warmth. It was like he had no memory of last night at the diner when they'd all bared their souls. Well, he hadn't bared his soul, but she and Cali had. It had been life-changing for her.

"Mmm, teensy bit over the limit?"

"You were going fifty in a thirty zone."

"Really? Huh." She worked on looking suitably surprised. "I'm very sorry about that. Won't happen again." She smiled, really hoping he'd let her off with a warning.

He remained cop-faced tough. "You put yourself and others in danger when you speed."

"Won't happen again. Promise." She widened her eyes and sent him an urgent telepathic message. *Friends don't give friends expensive tickets.*

He didn't get the message. "License and registration."

She made a valiant attempt to change the subject while complying with the hard-ass. "Do you enjoy working out?" she asked while she fetched the license and registration from the glove compartment.

"I lift weights, run, hike, and swim."

She handed him the requested items. "Wow! You're like a quadrathon athlete."

He stared at her driver's license. It wasn't the most flattering picture. She'd smiled and the guy had told her not to smile, so it had a weird half-frown, half-pursed-lip look. Also, her hair was frizzy from a terribly humid day.

"Never heard of a quadrathon," he muttered. He lifted his head, stared at her, and then looked at her license again. Like he wasn't sure if it was really the same person.

"I know it's not the best picture, but it's just me on a bad hair day. Anyway! Quadrathon athletes do four things. I made that up, but it seemed fitting. I bet you spend a lot of time at the gym." She tried not to notice since he was with Cali, but the man was *ripped* in the sexy way that appealed to all women everywhere. Massive shoulders, broad chest, and bulging biceps were clearly outlined in his short-sleeve blue cop shirt. Flat stomach too. For sure, she could bounce a quarter off those abs. And his forearms were tanned and ropey with muscle. She took all this in with a thoroughly objective eye, not a lusty haze, which was perfectly respectful of his couple status. Her gaze wandered lower to his utility belt full of cop gear and then lower to more…gear. She jerked her gaze back to his face and ordered her body to stop overheating. His face was quite handsome too—dark blue eyes, sharp cheekbones, clean-shaven square jaw softened by his full lips. If you weren't scared off by his hard expression, you might conclude he was a hottie of the highest degree.

His expression softened a bit. "I skip the gym since I've got weights at my place. I prefer outdoors for exercise." He abruptly turned and went back to his cruiser.

She sighed. She was definitely getting a ticket.

He returned a few minutes later and gave her a stern look. "You already have four points on your license for speeding. Two more points and you'll be required to go to a driver retraining program."

"Oh, Ethan, *please* don't give me a ticket. I was just excited to get my steps in." She held up her wrist. "Look, I got my

Fitness Mind today. Charlotte says I need ten thousand steps a day."

He gave her a dead-eye cop stare for so long she knew he was thinking about letting her off. She blinked frantic telepathic messages at him: *friends don't give friends tickets, friends don't give friends tickets.*

He handed back her license and registration. "You get a warning for today—"

"Thank you!"

"On two conditions."

"Anything."

"You swear never to speed again."

"I do, I swear!" She made a small cross over her heart. "Cross my heart and spit in my mother's eye."

He cracked a smile that catapulted him past hottie to spectacularly gorgeous. "That's not…never mind. That's fine. Other condition is, you get those steps in on a hike today with my hiking club."

"That's perfect! One of my new goals is to spend more time in nature. I've been so glued to the TV, my phone, and classroom work. In fact, I should get the kids out more too."

"Hike's one o'clock today at the reservation over in Fieldridge. I get off at noon. You want to go over together?"

She beamed. "Sure! Will Cali be there?"

He stared at her for a long moment. "I'll check in with her if you want. I mean, if you're not comfortable with just me." He leaned closer. "She's my partner."

She nodded once. Message received. It was rather enlightened the way Ethan called his girlfriend his partner. Obviously he had a great deal of respect for Cali. "Either way is good," she assured him. "Thanks again! You're a great cop."

He gave her a small almost shy smile. "I was recently promoted to sergeant. I could've taken the test earlier, but I wanted more experience before I supervised other cops. Course, I still do patrol work, but the pay's better."

It was the most he'd ever shared and she knew the promotion must've meant a lot to him. "Congratulations!"

He saluted. "Thank you, ma'am."

"Please don't call me ma'am."

"Will do. I'll pick you up at twelve thirty. Got the address from your license."

"Oh, wait! I recently moved. I'm in the apartment complex in Clover Park now." She rattled off the new address.

He returned to his hard-cop stare. "You need to file a change of address and update your license."

"Yes, sir! Keep up the good work, Sergeant Case!"

He shook his head, smiling, and headed back to his cruiser.

She blew out a breath, momentarily dazzled by his male beauty and forgiving nature. She quickly pulled down the visor and checked her look in the small mirror. Her eyes were dilated, her cheeks flushed with the damning evidence—lust. Worse, her hair was up in a messy ponytail and she was wearing the least sexy outfit she owned, an old gray T-shirt and purple and white polka dot leggings. She slammed the visor back in place, mad at herself for caring so much what she looked like. She reminded herself how great she felt with her new single me, happy me lifestyle. She would *not* be wasting time lusting over a guy, obsessing over a guy, or twisting herself into heights of painfully beautiful perfection (which was never perfect anyway). No man would be responsible for her happiness. She needed to learn to find her own happiness.

Besides, she guiltily reminded herself, Ethan was with Cali. She pulled her shirt away from her overheated body and fanned herself a bit. So, okay, her lusty hormones had perked up after an excruciatingly long dry spell, but that wasn't anything her vibrator couldn't take care of, right?

She glanced in the rearview mirror. Ethan was waiting for her to drive away first. Probably clocking her speed too. She drove off at a very sedate thirty miles per hour. An old man on a scooter could pass her at this rate. Ethan made a U-turn and headed in the opposite direction. She eased the acceleration a teensy bit faster. Close call with that speeding ticket, but it all turned out okay. And now she had another new hobby—hiking. Talk about expanding her horizons! Fitness, nature, what else could she do? Maybe she'd learn to be a gourmet cook, or start her own business on the side, making something cool no one ever thought of before, or maybe she'd learn ballroom dance or…pole dancing! Ooh, gardening, though that would have to wait until spring. Suddenly her whole life seemed full of possibilities!

She arrived home to her apartment, stepping inside to the empty quiet that still unsettled her. Setting her bags down, she took a deep breath. Now that she'd given up the fantasy of a romantic happy-ever-after, this could be her future, always coming home to emptiness. A life without love. She crossed her arms, hugging herself, and then with sheer determination, she pushed the dark despair down. No one ever said change was easy.

One step at a time.

She just had to believe she was worth it.

Ethan headed for Ally's apartment, walking at a brisker pace than he normally would to pick up a woman. She was just so damned appealing. He liked her easy cheerfulness, her big smiles, and natural enthusiasm for life. Sometimes he felt like he'd been born hard and jaded. Being around her was like breathing lighter air. He shook his head at himself and his unusually silly thoughts. He headed briskly upstairs to her third-floor apartment. All the hallways and staircases were open to the outside under a covered roof. He liked that, more fresh air circulating.

He rang the bell and the door popped open a minute later. Then he merely stared, speechless.

"Hi!" Ally said cheerfully. "I looked up hiking recommendations online and put together this outfit. You think it's good?"

This had to be a trick question. She looked utterly ridiculous in a large straw hat, white long-sleeved shirt tucked into khakis with white tube socks *over* the pants, pulled all the way up to her knees. Sneakers were fine.

He cocked his head. "Why're the socks *over* the pants?"

"Protection against ticks, silly. I'm wearing light colors so I can spot them more easily. Lyme disease is no joke." She looked at the ends of his jeans. "Here, let's fix your socks too."

"I'm good. I shower and check for ticks after the hike."

She stepped outside and locked the door behind her. He took in her adorably geeky self and decided he respected the fact that she cared more about protecting herself than what people thought of how she looked. It showed a certain confidence and fuck-all-the-haters attitude that he'd long ago embraced.

She headed downstairs, a small pink backpack bouncing on her back. "The website recommended a shower as well. I'll do that too."

He kept up with her, forcing his mind away from the tantalizing idea of showering together. "What's in the pack?"

"Water and a granola bar. Where's your backpack?"

"Left it in my Jeep."

"Let me guess, Gatorade and an extra-heavy pack for maximum workout."

He barked out a laugh because she was right. "Yup."

"How much weight?"

"Twenty pounds."

She shook her head and her big straw hat tipped. "I'm going to work up to that. How long is the hike anyway?"

"Usually runs from one to four."

She halted suddenly, grabbing his bicep before quickly dropping it. "Three hours! Are these advanced hikers?"

He lifted one shoulder. "Beginner to intermediate. We stop for hydration breaks. You can always follow the trail back to my Jeep if you get tired."

"Does anyone ever do that?"

He hesitated before admitting, "No."

She continued down the stairs. "I'm not going to be that weenie. Charlotte says I already have some nice muscle tone in my quads. I just need to work on my core and my arms."

He refrained from commenting on her body because he

wanted her way more than he had a right to at this stage in their relationship. But hell, she was lush with curves. He longed for softness pressed against him, though he'd never say that out loud. It would ruin his tough-cop image. Even her being a speed demon wasn't a deal breaker. She was just an enthusiastic person.

"Slow and steady build is better anyway," he said gruffly, not wanting to give away his lusty thoughts.

"How long did it take you to build strength? I mean, you're lugging around an extra twenty pounds on a three-hour hike."

The fact that she noticed his strength was a good sign. She'd been checking him out earlier too when he pulled her over. Some women had a thing for the uniform. "I've been working out since high school football days. Then I upped it for my job."

"Do you have to chase a lot of criminals?"

"You have to be prepared for any situation, but, yes, I've apprehended those who broke the law."

"Have you ever been shot?"

"I've been shot at, but never took a bullet. Eastman isn't a big haven for crime, but there's enough people to warrant a decent-size police force. Most problems center around drugs."

"Knock wood—" she knocked her head "—that you keep up that great record of never taking a bullet."

"Thanks."

She was quiet the rest of the way down the stairs. He wasn't sure if his job worried her or she was thinking of something else. There was really nothing to say that would reassure her about his job. It was what it was—long periods of not much going on, sudden high-risk situations. He handled it. And he liked that he could step in and right a wrong. He liked that people needed him most of all. It went a long way for someone who hadn't felt wanted or needed for way too long as a kid.

He gestured over to where he'd parked.

"I've seen this car a few times parked at Garner's. This is yours? Awesome!" She rushed over to the passenger side of his firecracker red Jeep Wrangler Unlimited. He loved his Jeep, the four-wheel drive was great in all terrain and off-road.

He opened the door for her and she hustled in.

"Will Cali be meeting us there?" she asked.

"No." He hadn't bothered to call her. He figured if Ally couldn't handle being alone with him on a short drive to a group hike, then she couldn't handle him at all. Better to know that up front. Some women found him too gruff. Maybe they wanted touchy-feely shit. That wasn't him.

"Oh," she said, her gaze fixed on his bicep. She jerked her gaze back to his eyes and smiled uncertainly. "Can we put the top down?"

"Yup." He shut the door. It wasn't a quick thing to take the soft top down, not if you did it right—taking out the side windows, back window, unlatching everything, pulling the roof back, storing everything safely in the back of the Jeep—but he'd make the effort for her. Several minutes later, he was satisfied that everything was safely stored and climbed in the driver's side.

"I had no idea it was that much work," she said. "Thanks for doing that."

"No problem." He started the Jeep and backed out of the space. "Hang onto your hat."

She took off the hat and rested it on her lap. Her hair remained flattened against her head and she ran her fingers through it, shaking it out. He wondered if it was as soft as it looked. Then she lifted her arms and wiggled her fingers out the top of the Jeep. "Whee-ee-ee!"

He chuckled at the reference to his partner's comically dry take on life and headed out to the main road.

"You have any other hobbies besides fitness?" she asked.

She was definitely interested in him. He played it cool. "Most of my time is spent at work or outdoors hiking, camping, fishing. I spend time with the guys too."

"Do you miss Zach?" That was his honorary brother he'd grown up with in the same foster home since they were nine.

They'd been the youngest boys there at the time, both orphans, and had stuck together. Other kids, mostly siblings, had passed through over the years, but only he and Zach stayed put. If it wasn't for Zach, Ethan wasn't sure he would've passed high school. Academics had never been his thing. Zach went on to get a PhD. Ethan did his part for Zach, making sure skinny Zach didn't get his ass kicked. Back then, Ethan would fight any guy that looked sideways at him. He'd been so pissed off for so long because no one wanted him enough to adopt him. He shuddered to think what would've become of him without Joe Campbell setting such a powerful example of what a man was, bringing him into the family, along with Zach, and making them feel like they belonged. Ethan didn't forget that kindness. He was, above all, loyal and remained firmly rooted in Eastman so he could be there not only for the family who'd taken him in, but also the community. He worked for the Eastman Police Department and coached football in the Police Athletic League that had been his haven as a kid.

He glanced over at Ally. "Why would I miss Zach? He lives in town now."

She waved airily. "Because, you know, now he's part of the Carrie-Zach couple unit. They're like all wrapped up in each other."

"Don't you see Carrie anymore?"

She sighed. "I do, but it's not the same. Her mind is in her studies, she just started graduate school, and the rest of the time she's with him. I mean, sure, I still see her at our book club meetings, a few special occasions, birthdays and stuff, but it's not the same."

Hanging out with Zach still felt exactly the same to him. They drank beer, played basketball, and razzed each other just like always. Women's relationships had a layer of complexity he had yet to crack.

"I mean, I'm happy for them," she said with forced cheer. "Yay, couplehood! But then what about yay, single friend, you know?"

He was about to ask if she wished she was part of a couple

too because it sure as hell sounded like that when she went on.

"Whatever," she sang. "I'm not bitter. I'm happy, happy, happy."

"Because of your single me, happy me plan?"

"Yes," she said firmly.

He mulled over how to make his case for being part of her happy-me plan minus the single, when she said in a voice full of warmth, "Thanks for not giving me a ticket."

It was something. A start. "Sure. Don't let it happen again."

"I sped a little on the way home."

"I didn't hear that."

"I jaywalk too. I just dart across the street the moment traffic clears."

He groaned. "Ally, seriously I'm going to have to take you through good citizenship one-oh-one."

"Like a dog?" She lifted her hands like paws and panted with her tongue out. "Train me up for my good citizenship. Arf! Bring lots of biscuits."

He smirked.

"You're thinking of doggy-style, aren't you?" she accused.

Already she was onto his dirty line of thinking. "I admit nothing. And please cross with the light. There's no reason to play chicken with traffic."

"You're kind of a goody-goody for a tough cop."

He glared at her. She laughed.

"You take that back," he ordered.

"Okay, okay, you just have an unhealthy respect for law and order."

He stopped at a red light and gave her his best intimidating cop stare. "I'm a frigging cop."

She put her palms up. "Don't arrest me, officer! It's not a crime to notice stuff about other people. Right? I mean, you're not on duty."

He clenched his jaw. He was the king of cool and *not* a goody-goody.

She patted his arm. "Lighten up. I'm just joking around."

He growled out his retort, giving it some bite. "Spend more time with me and you'll see just how much I'm not a goody-goody." He checked the light. Still red. He turned back to see her grinning.

"Challenge accepted. This'll be fun."

He grunted. Clearly she didn't find him too gruff. He liked that he wouldn't have to tiptoe around her tender feelings.

A short while later, he pulled into the gravel parking lot of the Fieldridge Reservation. Some of his hiking club was already there—a mix of people ranging from twenties to forties, just one couple, most of them were single. He figured once you were married with kids, you had less time for Sunday afternoon hikes. If he had a kid, he'd just strap him or her onto his back and take them with.

Ally hopped out of the Jeep before he could open her door. He met up with her.

She centered her hat on her head. "Introduce me to everyone."

He walked over with her and introduced her to the one married couple, George and Diana, then to some of the guys, Rob, Mike, and the two Matts. The women stared at her tick-resistant outfit. All the women wore jeans and long-sleeve shirts. Nobody wore a hat. All socks were under their pant cuffs where they belonged.

He gestured toward the women. "This is Trina, Hillary, Becky, Sarah," he paused, squinting as he tried to remember the last one.

"Maria," she supplied.

"Yes, Maria. Sorry. Not great with names. This is Ally, first-time hiker."

"I've hiked before," Ally said with a grin. "The mall is my preferred venue, but I read up on hiking and I'm all set."

The women looked her up and down. "That's good," someone mumbled.

"It's to keep ticks away," Ally explained, pointing to her socks. "And light colors to make it easier to spot them."

That launched everyone on their own tale of Lyme disease. Many people had been exposed, but if you pulled the tick off within twenty-four hours, you were usually safe. Caught early, antibiotics took care of it. Caught late, it was a long haul to recovery.

"See, Ethan?" Ally said, giving him a poke to the shoulder. "I told you it was important."

"You did."

More people showed up. Eight guys, six women. Their fearless leader, Rob, a crunchy guy with long brown dreads in a loose bun, announced they'd waited long enough and the rest of the group could catch up on the trail. Or as he put it, "You snoozed, you probably boozed." He had lots of pithy expressions involving alcohol and pot.

At first, Ethan walked with Ally, but her stride was so much shorter and her pace so slow, it became almost painful to keep stride with her. She waved him on, already out of breath thirty minutes in. It was a gradual uphill climb.

"Do your thing," she panted. "I'll catch up."

"Sure?"

"Yes, I'll be fine."

A half hour later, Ally trailing increasingly behind the group, they all stopped for a hydration break. It was a good stopping place in a small clearing with some flat boulders to rest on. He crossed to her side where she sat leaning against a tree.

"You doing okay?" he asked.

She nodded and took a long drink of water.

He dropped his pack and stretched. He loved a hard physical workout; something he'd learned in high school was better all around for everyone. It focused his energy and dramatically decreased the number of fistfights he got in. He chugged some Gatorade and watched Ally.

She took off her hat and fanned herself with it. He hated to say it, but she looked completely exhausted. She was sweating, cheeks flushed pink, hair flattened in scraggly blond locks around her cute pixie face. She wasn't used to hiking.

"Jeep's unlocked," he told her. "Why don't you head back and rest? I'll meet you back there."

She eyed him. "I am *not* a weenie."

He grinned. "At the end of this trail is a nice view—a huge lake surrounded by trees."

"Describe it for me. Make it real. I need the motivation."

"Sure." He looked off in the distance, trying to bring it all into focus from memory. "Well, the water is blue with light ripples. Plenty of fish—lotta trout, small mouth, yellow perch. Sometimes you'll see a turtle sunning itself on a log. This time of year, the trees are just starting to turn color around the edges of the lake, bright reds, oranges, and yellows. Blue sky that seems to meet the treeline. So much sky, feels like a bigger sky there." He kept going, remembering tons of little details. He'd spent a lot of time at this lake, fishing and camping. "You'll love it," he finally concluded, turning back to her.

She was asleep.

He admired her for a moment, geeky tube socks and all. What a fighter, working herself to the point of exhaustion. Now he had two choices, give her a piggyback ride to the end of the trail or help her back to the Jeep. The view was spectacular. She'd probably feel like a weenie sitting in the Jeep.

He nudged her arm. "Wake up, there's an awesome view with your name on it."

She kept sleeping.

He squatted next to her, took her water bottle from her limp hand, and plucked her hat off her lap. He fanned her with the hat. "Ally," he barked, "up and at 'em, soldier."

"Omigod!" one of the women exclaimed. "She fell asleep?"

Ethan straightened. "She's not used to a strenuous workout. This is her second one today." He nudged Ally's leg with his foot. "Come on, wake up."

The other hikers gathered around, looking at her curiously. "Has she been sick?" someone asked.

"No, she's fine." He loosened the cap on her water bottle and dripped some cold water over her head.

She startled awake, peered up at him still holding the water bottle over her head, and scrambled to her feet, snatching the water bottle from him with an unholy gleam in her eyes.

4

Splash! Right in his face.

"Hey!" he exclaimed with a laugh. "Someone give me water. I need ammunition." All he had was Gatorade.

Someone tossed water at his back. He turned and suddenly a water war broke out, everyone laughing and squealing as the cold water hit. It was nuts and probably the most fun their group had ever had.

Finally they were completely out of ammunition. He turned back to Ally to find her pulling her now see-through soaked white shirt away from her body. She might as well have been standing there naked in her bra, her nipples beaded tight, luscious large breasts clearly outlined. His mouth went dry.

"Wet T-shirt contest," she quipped.

And while he damn well appreciated the view, he could tell she was embarrassed. They still had another couple of hours on the trail.

He pulled his T-shirt off and offered it to her. "Here, it's only wet in the back. We'll put your shirt in the sun on one of the rocks, and when we get back, it should be closer to dry."

She stared at his chest, her gaze trailing to his abs. He waited for her to meet his eyes. Hers were wide and dilated. *Nice.*

He pressed his shirt into her hand. "Go into the woods to change. I'll wait for you."

"Are those twelve-pack abs?" she croaked.

He looked down at himself. "Six-pack, I think."

She gestured near his sides. "But there's like ridges and *wow*."

He smiled. He liked wow.

"Heading out!" Rob called. Everyone started gathering their packs and putting away their empty water bottles.

"Hurry up and change," he told Ally.

She stared at him, her voice soft. "You gave me the shirt off your back."

"It was the only one I had."

She rushed forward and hugged him. It was so fast he didn't get a chance to hug her back. She pulled away and hurried behind a large sugar maple tree. "Thanks!"

He just stood there in a warm and fuzzy daze.

She returned in his shirt, which hung low like a dress on her. Something primitive in his brain lit up with a possessive streak he'd never felt before. Like he'd claimed her.

"Where should I put this?" she asked, wringing out her white shirt.

He forced himself to focus. "I got it." He spread it over a rock he knew would have full sun for a while longer.

"Last one there's gotta jump in the lake!" she said, grabbing her pack and taking off.

He shook his head. That would be a several-hundred-foot dive into the lake, but he had to admire her fortitude. He grabbed his pack, the huge hat she forgot, and caught up with her easily. He could hear their group, now cheerfully talking after their refreshing water war, but he couldn't see them. They really should catch up.

"You want a piggyback ride to the summit?" he asked, setting her hat on her head. "It's no problem. You'll keep the sun off my back."

She frowned. "Maybe we should've put my wet shirt on your back for sun protection."

"Nah, I've got a good tan from the summer, I'm used to it. Besides, we'll be back in the shade trees before you know it."

Her gaze dropped to his chest and then lower before jerking back to his eyes, her cheeks flushing pink. "You're so…" She cleared her throat. "I mean, dang, I'm so embarrassed how much more fit you are than me."

She wants me.

"Everyone starts somewhere." He strapped his pack on backwards onto his chest, turned and bent down. "Climb on."

"I weigh more than a hundred pounds, you know."

He glanced at her over his shoulder. She was staring at his back and he couldn't tell if she was tempted to climb on or just checking him out some more. "I'm aware fully grown adults normally do."

"You're saying you can hike with a hundred pounds on your back?"

"I could do more. Come on. We're losing daylight."

She walked around to stand in front of him. "I want to be you when I come back as a tough guy."

He laughed and sprang to his feet.

She waved him on. "Keep going, tough guy. I'll do this my own way. Slow, but I'll get there."

He tweaked her hat. "Slow and steady has a lot of integrity."

"Yeah, yeah."

"I'll wait for you at the summit. If you're not there within a half hour, I'm coming back for you."

"There won't be a search and rescue, geez!" She adjusted her hat and spoke through her teeth. "I…can…do…this."

He put his palms up and headed back on the trail at his usual pace. Far be it from him to get in the way of a determined woman. He admired the hell out of her grit.

He caught up with the group, keeping his ears open for the sound of a determined woman collapsing on the trail behind him. Next thing he knew, they were in the clearing at the summit. The view took his breath away like always—blue sky as far as the eye could see, the wide expanse of lake reflecting the sky, the surrounding trees lit with afternoon sun in an explosion of colors—green, yellow, red, and orange. He inhaled deeply, at peace. Moments like this he believed, contrary to all of his experiences, that the world was a good place.

He turned back to the trail and looked for Ally. Several minutes passed in silence except for the sound of the group behind him eating and joking around. They often ate a healthy snack at the halfway point. He'd wait for Ally to eat his. He'd brought two apples, one for him, one for her.

He heard her before he saw her, her feet heavy like she was trudging along. It took everything he had not to scoop her up to give her some relief.

Finally she came into view. The moment she saw him, her face broke into a wide smile and she threw her arms in the air. "I did it!"

"Sure did," he managed over the lump in his throat. Her small victory touched him for reasons he couldn't comprehend. It wasn't like *he* did anything. He was just so happy for her.

She made her slow way over to him. "I guess I'm the one who has to jump in the lake."

"Nah. Much too big a fall. C'mon." He jerked his head for her to follow. When they reached the best viewing spot, almost but not quite at the edge, he whispered, "Check it out. Your reward for all that hiking."

She sucked in air. "Oh! It's just like you described. Breathtakingly beautiful."

He took in the view with her. "It is."

After a few minutes, she turned to him. "Please tell me there's a rest period before we hike back down."

"Yes, and downhill is a lot easier. You hungry?"

She nodded.

He gestured for her to follow him to a flat boulder and offered her an apple.

"Thanks," she said, taking a big bite. "This is better than a granola bar."

"Agreed." He ate his apple and kept an eye on her for signs of falling asleep. She was actually perky, bright-eyed, looking around as she chomped the apple enthusiastically. Fighter all the way. Something in the vicinity of his heart shifted. He *really* liked her.

Some of the other hikers came over to fist-bump her and congratulate her for conquering her first hike.

"Still have to make it back," Ally said.

"You got this," one of the Matts said. "This is a tough trail for a first-timer. Your boyfriend should've told you that."

Ally smiled and crinkled her nose. "We're just friends."

Matt checked in with him and Ethan narrowed his eyes. Matt smirked and Ethan's hackles rose. He stood to face Matt eye to eye, man to man. *Seriously going to move in on the woman wearing my shirt in front of me?*

Matt turned and walked away. *Thought so.*

Ethan sat next to Ally and finished his apple in three fierce bites.

"What was that about?" Ally asked.

"I didn't appreciate his smirk."

"You smirk all the time."

"Not like that."

"Oh-kay." She finished up her apple. "Where should I throw this away?"

"We take out whatever we take in. Here." He held out his palm.

"You want my chewed apple core? My slobber is all over it."

He laughed. "I'll live."

She gingerly placed it in his palm.

"Ah!" he exclaimed. "Girl cooties!"

She laughed. "Tough guy does have a sense of humor!"

He tucked the apple cores into a sandwich bag in his pack. "Not as good as say, a knock-knock joke, but ya know…"

"Hey, some of my knock-knock jokes are very funny."

"To first graders."

She poked his shoulder. "To everyone, tough guy."

He met her eyes. "Tough girl. I'm impressed with how hard you worked to get here. Some people would've taken the easy way out and gone back to civilization."

"Weenies all!" she declared.

He found himself smiling again. He couldn't remember ever smiling so much. "Got that right. I honestly didn't think it was that hard a trail. Sorry if I underestimated it."

"I'm fine."

"You're probably going to be sore tomorrow. Take a day to rest your muscles."

"I will, thanks." She bumped her shoulder into his.

He bumped her back and then had to grab her before she tipped off the boulder. "You're a lightweight."

She smiled sunnily. "That is the nicest thing a guy has ever said to me. It's nice having a guy friend." She stood and stretched, arching her back in his blue shirt, her breasts full and tempting.

Guy friend. Not for long. He smirked, picturing her in his shirt after a roll in the sheets, prancing around his townhouse, bare underneath.

She didn't notice his smirk, instead walking over to admire the view again. He admired her rear view, his shirt clinging to her cute ass.

On the way back down, Ally trailed behind again. He knew she'd be okay. She'd get there in her own time. He whistled to himself on the way down, enjoying sharing one of his favorite activities with Ally. She'd only improve as she got stronger. Maybe they could go on some trails just the two of them.

He stopped off for her shirt, which was still damp, and tied it to the straps of his pack, letting it dry over the back of the pack. He reached the parking lot and waited. And waited. She finally emerged, smiling and chatting with their leader, dreadlock Rob. The guy must've doubled back for her because he was always at the front of their group.

He met up with them just in time to hear Rob asking for Ally's number.

She smiled and shook her head. "Sorry, I'm seeing someone, but thanks."

Rob met his eyes. "Sorry, man. Matt said you were just friends. That's cool."

"No worries," Ally assured Rob. "Ethan and I are just friends. It's somebody else."

Rob shot him a confused look before turning back to Ally. "Hope to see you back with the group. Very nice to meet you."

"You too!" she said cheerfully.

Ethan clenched his jaw. What the hell? She was seeing someone after all that commitment to singlehood talk? He turned and headed back to his Jeep and Ally followed, patting his backpack.

"My shirt's still pretty wet," she said. "You mind if I hang onto your shirt until the next time I see you?"

"No problem," he muttered.

"Do you have an extra shirt in your car?"

"Just a hoodie. I'm fine like this." He would continue to go shirtless as long as Ally continued to ogle him. He calmed down a little. She must've been giving Rob a line, right? She'd been going on about her single me, happy me plan on the way over here.

They reached his Jeep and he opened the passenger-side door for her. She climbed in and turned to him, her gaze glued to his face. "You want to put the roof back on? I don't want you to get chilly."

Real men didn't get chilly.

"I'm fine." He headed over to the driver's side, started the Jeep, and looked over at her. She had a small smile playing over her lips. "Enjoy yourself?"

She beamed. "I did. There's something about being in nature that just makes you feel at peace. Like all is right in the world."

"Yes." He relaxed because she really appreciated what he'd shown her here today. He put the Jeep in gear and pulled out of the lot. It wasn't like he had a claim on her. Of course men were going to hit on her. She was beautiful, sexy and sweet, lit from within from some exuberant life force. Oh, man, he had it bad. He had to make a move soon before another guy moved in. But wait, maybe another guy already had.

He glanced over at her to find her staring at his chest. Her eyes met his, the expression somewhere between lust and guilt. Did she feel guilty because she was secretly seeing someone? If that was the case, then what the hell was with all that single me, happy me talk?

"Who're you seeing?" he asked casually. "I was just wondering because it's only been a day since your commitment to singlehood."

She laughed. "I'm seeing myself. I want to focus on my life. I wasted too much energy on relationships, you know? Now my relationship is with myself."

He smirked. "I bet you have a great sex life."

"Excuse me?"

His attempt at humor had flatlined. "I mean, you're in a relationship with yourself, so you know exactly what you like."

"Oh, I guess so!"

They laughed.

"Sorry if that was inappropriate," he said.

"Not at all! I love inappropriate. I always say a vibrator is better than a man and it's true!"

"No—" he started.

"You're actually really funny." Her gaze wandered from his bare shoulder to his bicep. "I don't remember you being funny before today." Her voice came out hoarse and she cleared her throat.

He dropped his voice to a husky tone. "I think the *right* man would definitely be better than a vibrator."

A moment of charged silence.

He glanced over at her staring at him, lips parted, eyes wide. He winked.

She sucked in air. "Well, that's not—I mean, I don't…"

He chuckled, low and dirty.

"Of course a man would say that," she retorted. "Men *vastly* overestimate their prowess, no offense."

"Whenever someone says no offense, they mean offense."

"No, really, no offense." She stared straight ahead, smoothing her hair. "So how come you're funny today and not when I saw you before, you know, at Garner's for drinks with the guys, parties and stuff."

"Usually I'm tired when you see me after pulling some long shifts. Today was an easy morning." He paused and then just decided to go for it. "So hiking club meets every other Sunday. You want to go again? Or we could go sooner, just the two of us."

She spoke quickly, the words tumbling over each other. "I'll let you know. I've got a lot of things I want to try. I need to keep my options open. How's Cali doing?"

He deflated. "She's fine." Keeping options open sounded like a no to him, but he didn't give up that easy. "You did say you enjoyed yourself today and you'll only get better the more you hike. I'll give you my number, so text or call, whatever, if you change your mind." He waited while she pulled out her phone, and spoke slowly and clearly as he told her his number. Then he told her to text him so he knew she had it right, which was mostly so he could get her number. He'd check it once he parked.

"Aww, you are cold!" She rubbed his arm and he warmed at the spot. "Look, you've got goose bumps."

"Maybe a little," he admitted, hoping she'd keep touching him. He had a lot of skin exposed, being shirtless and all. Her fingers wandered the shape of his arm from shoulder to elbow, her touch soft, until she suddenly seemed to realize what she was doing and snatched her hand back.

He smiled. That felt like a yes.

5

———

Ethan knew it wasn't the subtlest of moves showing up at the Happy Endings Book Club meeting for the sole purpose of running into Ally, but he figured the more he saw her, the more chances he had of hooking her interest. It had been four days and he hadn't heard from her about going on another hike, but that could mean she just didn't want to go hiking again. Nothing against him. He went to the counter of Something's Brewing Café and ordered some coffee to go. He couldn't stay long. He was in uniform on his way for a night shift. One of the guys had called out sick because his wife was in labor. Ethan was one of the few single cops on staff and didn't mind picking up some overtime. Even if he didn't have to work, there was no way he'd stay long enough to actually participate in a girly romance book club. His goal was simple, see Ally and exchange a brief hello.

His coffee was served up by the red-haired owner, Shane O'Hare. "Thanks, Shane. Your coffee is the best."

Shane smiled. "That's our new house blend, all fair-trade, organic."

"I'm sure it's fantastic." He turned at the sound of women's laughter as they filed in, walking close in the way women friends did. He spotted Ally right away with the blond Carrie. They could pass as sisters and seemed as close as ever to him. Ally wore a soft-looking light blue sweater that clung to her beautiful breasts with black jeans and canvas high-top sneakers—one red, one green. He loved that quirkiness.

Ally spotted him and rushed over. "Looks like I have a stalker." She smiled cheekily.

He smiled back. You'd have to be a corpse not to return one of Ally's smiles. "I was here first. Maybe you're stalking me."

She tossed her hair. "This is our book club night, you know."

He tugged a lock of her hair. "And does your book club discriminate against men?"

She bit back a smile. "That depends if men enjoy reading hot romance. Hmm?" Her blue eyes danced with good humor, like she knew she'd got him.

He smirked, his mind already going to men *acting out* hot romance when Hailey, the leader of the book club and notorious matchmaking wedding planner, suddenly appeared at his side. He casually eased away from her. Hailey had pulled out all the stops flirting with him last month in a heavyhanded attempt to prove he was not a sex addict, but actually great boyfriend material. Though it was clear she wasn't interested in him, more like her flirting was for the benefit of everyone around them. He'd felt steamrolled.

Hailey beamed at him. "We'd love to have you. We've been trying to get more men in here from day one. The male perspective on romance could be very useful."

He eased back another step. "I'm probably not the guy you're looking for."

He and Ally exchanged a smile. He lifted his to-go cup. "Back to work. Enjoy your book club."

"Bye!" Ally wiggled her fingers at him.

He wiggled his fingers back and quickly dropped his hand, embarrassed at the wimpy gesture. He turned and resumed his usual tough-cop swagger out the door.

It was a strange situation he'd found himself in. He could see competing with another man for a woman's attention, but to compete against a woman's attention to herself was a much trickier situation.

Hell, he lived for a challenge. *Bring it on, Ally. Let's both pay attention to your sexy self. Maybe then you'll believe a man is better than a vibrator.*

He smirked and got into his cruiser.

Ally settled into her seat in the circle of women at the Happy Endings Book Club meeting at Something's Brewing Café, a cozy space with dark wood tables, deep red walls, and golden sconces around the hanging lights. The nine of them sat in the center of the room, the tables pushed to the edges.

She was bursting to share. She crossed her leg, resting her ankle on the knee of the other leg, and then gripped the black jeans over her calf with both hands, waiting for a lull in the conversation. Finally, she got her moment and boldly declared her new philosophy. "These stories are escapist fantasy. I love them, but it's no longer anything I expect for myself."

She waited breathlessly for the explosion of protests. She'd just rocked the foundation of what the Happy Endings Book Club stood for. These were her closest friends, a sisterhood founded on their shared love of romance. Everyone loved the happy endings. Everyone wanted that for themselves.

Silence. Everyone stared at her.

Oh-kay, perhaps further explanation was necessary. "I'm no longer looking for a man to bring me my happy-ever-after. I take responsibility for my own happiness."

"With you, girl," Missy, a tough practical woman, replied. She'd recently dyed her beautiful red hair back to dark brown and it made her look even more tough and serious. "I only read these books for the hot sex."

"Me too," Lexi declared. She was a vivacious, terribly-jaded-about-men corporate event planner. "Like a happy-ever-after is real," she scoffed.

"I used to feel the same way," Mad declared. This was

not surprising. Mad was the youngest and only girl in the Campbell family and a total tomboy. Mad leaned forward in her V-neck T-shirt, giving them all a peek at the hawk tattoo above her heart. "But, ladies, happy-ever-after kind of love *is* real. I've got it with Park. I've never been so happy in my life."

Everyone got quiet. The group was now about evenly split between single women and coupled women, and Ally felt that divide even more keenly.

Hailey, their fearless leader, looking radiant as ever in a designer tan A-line dress with matching heels, spoke up. "We can agree to disagree on the truth of these stories we all love. But remember—" she paused, queen of the dramatic pause "—sometimes love blooms where we least expect it."

Ally leaned forward, shoving her blond bangs out of her eyes. "What ever happened to Make Love Bloom (TM)?" That had been Hailey's fledgling matchmaking program with another book club member, now happily engaged in spite of Hailey's efforts.

Hailey huffed and smoothed nonexistent wrinkles from her dress. "I just decided to let things happen more naturally. With a little assist when needed." She gave them all a small smile.

They all stared at Hailey in shock. This went against everything the woman had stood for in the two years their book club had been meeting. Hailey was a self-proclaimed love junkie and happy-ending facilitator. Why was she backing off after making it her mission to see every one of them coupled up for their very own happy ending?

"Did something happen, Hailey?" Ally asked gently. "Did you get together with someone or break up? What brought on this new attitude?"

Hailey flicked her long strawberry blond hair over her shoulder. "Nothing happened. I just realized a subtler approach might be more comfortable for everyone." She stared at the floor for a moment, an unusually subdued expression on her face. She looked up suddenly and pasted on her beauty-queen smile. She was a former beauty queen and that smile popped up in high-stress situations. "Ready to begin with chapter one, ladies?"

"Sure," Ally said, giving her an out. Hailey always liked to read chapter one of each new story out loud with the group so they could experience it together. She was quite a good actress too, acting out all the voices.

Hailey stood and began reading from her e-reader, chapter one of *Second Chance Love*. Ally had been the one to suggest the story, excited at the time about her own second chance at love with Dean. Now, not so much. Her mind wandered to running into Ethan. She hadn't seen him since the hike four days ago. Not like she counted the days to see him again. It had been…nice to see him. He'd smelled amazing—woodsy and clean—and he'd looked so solid and sexy in his uniform. Those wide shoulders and muscular arms, that chest. His gorgeous smile that lit up his face. She felt herself flush.

Oh, God, I'm a terrible person. Here she was committed to a new single me, happy me lifestyle and she was lusting after another woman's boyfriend. Augh. What was wrong with her? Why couldn't she just enjoy singlehood? Her mom's impassioned speech about the dangers of giving yourself too freely and to the wrong man came to mind, cooling her lust. Impulsive lusty tendencies had painful consequences. Her gut twisted at the memory she'd never shared with anyone.

She forced herself to focus on her friends, who she knew would help her stay strong in her resolve to make the most of singlehood, and sipped her cafe mocha, her regular indulgence at book club. She'd missed her favorite drink this past month. Ever since former book club member and movie star, Claire Jordan, arrived back in town to film the last movie in the Fierce trilogy, *Fierce Loving*, they'd all been meeting in a private lounge in Claire's hotel in Manhattan on Saturday nights. This was a necessity for Claire's personal safety and privacy. She was wildly popular with men and women alike as well as the paparazzi. Claire couldn't make it to book club this week, so they were back at their old meeting spot in the café. After the meeting, they'd head across the street to Garner's Sports Bar & Grill for drinks. It should be interesting to see how Josh, the bartender and manager of Garner's, reacted to seeing Hailey, his ultimate frenemy, again. Would the pair pick up right where they left off, or would the month-long separation cool the angst between them? Either way, they were bound to be entertaining—both of them experts at the stealth underhanded move. Ally's personal favorite? Hailey's rumor that Josh was impotent, which she squashed at his insistence by implying the problem was really a tiny banana. Josh had then spread the news that they used to date and Hailey believed he was the one that got away. The zingers they got in! Sometimes it was like watching one of those old black-and-white screwball romantic comedies. Ally had watched a few at Hailey's recommendation.

Hailey finished her dramatic reading, took her seat, and asked, "What do you think?"

Sabrina sighed dreamily. "I do love a good second-chance romance. It's like fate brings them together. They're just meant to be." She was a relationship counselor, so naturally an advocate of reunited lovers. She had the most compassionate nature, her brown eyes seemed soulful, and her round apple cheeks and long dirty-blond hair gave her a girl-next-door approachability. Damn. She should've checked in with Sabrina about Dean before getting herself so worked up over the reunion. What a waste of Ally's valuable time.

"Fate," Missy spat. "Please. No such thing. You really think there's some magical force bringing people together?"

"It seems that way sometimes," Sabrina said diplomatically. "For some people."

The women got into a heated debate over fate and the possibility of soul mates. There were a surprisingly high number of votes for fate. In fact, only Missy and Lexi were staunch skeptics. Ally used to be in the lovely fantasy of fate camp. Now she rejected the romantic notion. She made her own fate, her own destiny.

The conversation veered to chatty, everyone updating each other on all the latest. Ally kept quiet, her thoughts purposefully veering away from her friends' weddings, engagements, pregnancy, all things that were not part of her life, and focused on how good she felt with her new fitness regimen. And how good she was becoming at taking care of herself, seeking her own happiness with fulfilling experiences.

She jolted as Carrie, her former roomie with bright blond hair that fell in soft layers just past her jaw, called from across the circle, "We haven't heard from you, Ally. How'd it go with Dean at the reunion?" She smiled encouragingly. The reunion was less than a week ago and Ally had valiantly tried to push the disastrous outcome from her mind in favor of focusing on the good that had come from it. Carrie knew all about Ally's foolish drive to reconnect with her lost love.

"Not well," Ally replied tightly.

"I'm sorry," Carrie said softly. "Didn't mean to bring up a painful topic."

Ally lifted her chin. "It didn't work out with Dean. Our time is over. But you know what? I'm just fine with that. I discovered—" she shook her head ruefully "—a little late in the game, but I finally discovered that I am enough. I make my own happiness and I depend on no man for that. I was sold a bill of goods that a prince would show up and transform my life into happy-ever-after. I've dropped that fantasy. I'm on a mission to make my life the happiest it can be on my own."

She startled when the women broke out in applause, even the coupled women. And then she beamed because her sisters were clearly on her side.

"Hear, hear," Hailey said, raising a fist in the air. "Let's head over to Garner's and toast to that."

The women gathered their purses and headed out the door. Several women gave her arm a squeeze and told her she had the right idea. Even dopey-in-love Carrie said, "I'm so happy you're focusing on you. I worried how much you'd invested in Dean. This is the right path for you. I can tell by the enthusiasm in your voice. I predict great things!"

"Thanks," Ally said, giving Carrie's arm a squeeze. She hadn't realized Carrie worried over Ally's investment in

Dean. She supposed, Carrie not knowing Dean, she'd just hoped for the best.

The women arrived at the crowded bar full of couples and plenty of guys drinking beer and watching whatever sport that was on the TVs hanging above the dark cherrywood bar. She squinted. Baseball? Who cared? She no longer had to pretend to be interested in sports because that was one of those ways she'd twisted herself just to hang with a guy. Now she focused on her interests.

A tall man in a blue Henley and jeans turned from the bar and crossed to them. "Ladies," he said, "long time no see." It looked like Josh Campbell, which was weird because he was usually behind the bar. His dark brown hair was cut shorter, his deep brown eyes warm, charming smile as usual.

But then Hailey beamed, which she would never do with Josh. "Jake! Great to see you!" She gave him a brief hug.

That explained it. Jake and Josh were identical twins and Ally couldn't tell them apart. It might've been Josh with a haircut. She looked past some tall people and finally spotted Josh behind the bar, pouring a glass of water with lemon that he promptly put in front of pregnant Charlotte. He took extra special care of her because they were family now. Charlotte had married Josh's younger brother Ty.

Jake greeted each of them warmly. "Claire wishes she could've met with you this week. Her schedule shifted to nights and she needs to sleep as much as possible days. The camera is very unforgiving." Jake was Claire's husband.

The women all murmured instant forgiveness and asked Jake to say hi to Claire for them.

Jake returned to his seat at the bar and Josh appeared in front of him, grumbling something. Josh looked up and locked eyes with Hailey.

Hailey's lips parted, her gaze fixed on Josh.

Interesting. Maybe they missed each other?

Hailey approached the bar and Ally followed, hoping for a front-row view.

"Hi, Josh," Hailey said softly.

"Hey," Ally called cheerfully.

Josh glanced at Ally, jerked his chin, and returned his gaze to Hailey. "Princess, finally gracing us with your royal presence."

Hailey actually blushed. Normally she took offense to the princess remarks. "We've been meeting in the city with Claire."

"Yeah, Jake told me. Top-secret location with security. Didn't mean you couldn't stop by. You work just down the road."

"I've been—"

"Busy," Josh finished for her.

Hailey smoothed her hair. "Yes."

"Completely understand being busy," Josh said, grabbing a rag and scrubbing the bar top. "I've been really busy too."

Hailey let out a small forced laugh. "Guess we're both really busy."

An awkward silence fell.

Hailey backed away. "I need to check in with Lauren about her wedding."

"Gotta do what you gotta do," Josh said, not bothering to look up.

"Yes. So…" Hailey lifted a hand, her fingers fluttering in a small goodbye.

Josh looked up and raised his brows in response. He wasn't a finger flutterer. Hailey headed over to the back of the group with Lauren.

That was weird.

Josh stared at the bar top.

Ally sat next to Jake. "So how's the glam Hollywood life?" Jake worked for Claire's production company now, so he was even more involved.

Jake laughed. "Not as glam as you'd think." He looked over her shoulder. "Ethan! Get your ass over here!"

Ally turned to find Ethan dressed in regular clothes— white T-shirt and jeans—instead of his uniform. My God, he filled out that shirt nicely. She flushed, embarrassed at her uncontrollable admiration for his incredibly muscled form, but unable to tear her gaze away.

Ethan crossed to them, winked at Ally, and threw an arm around Jake's neck in a quick hug. "Finally slumming with us regular folk."

Jake socked Ethan in the gut, who socked him back, the pair of them grinning at each other. "Been too long, man," Jake said. "What's new in copland?"

"He got promoted to sergeant," Ally put in.

Ethan gifted her with a smile that brought warmth to those blue eyes and a tender expression to his gorgeous face. Her stomach fluttered in a crazy dance of lust, her skin hot, every part of her hyperaware of him. "Sure did," he said warmly.

"That's great," Jake said. "Congratulations. Let me buy you a drink."

"Sure, thanks." Ethan shifted to stand next to her at the bar. "You stalking me again?"

She laughed. "This time I was here first. You done work already?"

"Turned out the guy I stepped in for reported to work after all. Just a little late. His wife's labor was a false alarm." He stared at her hair, then her cheeks, her neck, and her lips. Warmth spread everywhere his gaze touched, bringing a low ache in her belly. "Buy you a drink?"

She licked her lips, leaning closer, every nerve tingling in anticipation. Then she remembered his girlfriend.

She eased back a bit. "How's Cali?"

He smirked. "Great. Living it up in Rio de Janeiro."

The smirk meant he was thinking dirty, but his girlfriend was getting dirty without him. Weird. "She didn't invite you on vacation with her?"

They stared at each other.

Something wasn't adding up.

"Hold up," Ethan said, a slow smile dawning. "Ally, she's my *partner*."

Ally huffed and lifted her palms to show him she was hands-off. "I know she's your partner. I get it, okay?"

He smiled even more. "I mean my actual partner at work."

"At work," she echoed, her mind whirling. She wasn't a terrible person after all. Relief quickly morphed into anger. He might've been clearer about him and Cali. She'd felt so guilty lusting over his manly self. If she had any sense at all, she'd pull herself out of this vortex of lusty attraction and make some serious space between her and Ethan.

Sense had never been her strong suit.

She eased closer again. He smelled wonderful like the outdoors, all woodsy earthy sex appeal. "But she wasn't with you when you pulled me over for speeding."

His dark blue eyes were hot on hers, his voice husky. "I picked up someone else's shift that day."

"Or tonight," she breathed.

He rested his arm on the bar top behind her and it was almost like he'd put his arm around her, hot and close. The wave of lust made her nearly woozy; electricity raced through her, heart pounding, skin hot. It had been way too long.

His voice was gravelly, close enough to give her a shiver. "She's in Brazil for two weeks, so you're not going to see us working together anytime soon. Now can I buy you a drink?"

She was tempted, so tempted. She was the designated driver for her friends tonight, though it was early enough she could probably swap with someone. It would be so easy. Have a few drinks, fall into bed, but then what? It was too soon to get caught up in a sex cocktail. Not that he'd offered a sex cocktail, but her body was getting that message loud and clear. Deep down she knew why she hadn't been with a man in a long while and it was reason enough for her brain to call a halt to her body's urgings.

And she needed to stop hoping for a fantasy man to make her life all sunshine and roses. Even if Ethan was very close to her ideal fantasy man—all gorgeous with a sense of humor and generous nature.

She waved in the direction of her friends. "I'm the desig-nated driver for the apartment crowd. I'm in the same complex as Missy, Lexi, and Sabrina. Just water for me tonight and that's free. Thanks, anyway."

Josh served up Ethan's beer and coughed out, "Crash and burn."

Ally froze.

Ethan smirked at Josh. "Sorry, did you say you wanted to see Hailey? Where is that tempting princess?"

Josh's gaze went right to Hailey like he kept track of her. Ethan and Jake laughed. Ally bit back a smile.

"Notice how he knew right where she was?" Ethan asked Jake.

"Messed up," Jake said.

"Shut up or you're both cut off," Josh growled.

Ally left the three of them razzing each other and made her escape, meeting up with Carrie. She'd missed her since they didn't live together anymore. Sisters before misters was her new mantra.

When her friends were ready for her to drive them back to the apartment complex, she said her goodbyes to the other ladies and sent a wave in the general direction of the guys. Ethan gave her a small ironic salute. She saluted back and sailed out the door.

Ally drove her ancient white Ford Escort, it had been her older sister's car, with Missy in the passenger seat, Lexi and Sabrina in the back. She'd just pulled out to Main Street when Missy surprised her with a sweet compliment. "I really admired what you said at book club tonight."

Ally glanced over at her. "Thank you! I really meant it. This commitment to myself is so eye-opening. I realized I need to learn to trust myself, to give *myself* an incredible life, to accept my flaws and work on improving my strengths." She'd given this a lot of thought, actually. Now that she'd resisted temptation, she was more committed than ever.

"Beautiful," Missy murmured.

"That's a thing!" Sabrina piped up from the backseat. "I mean, committing to yourself. It's called sologamy. You can marry yourself."

The hair on the back of Ally's neck stood at attention. "Marry myself?"

"Yes! It symbolizes commitment to self," Sabrina said.

"You guys!" Ally exclaimed. "I've got goose bumps. I'm doing it! I'm marrying myself. I'm going to get a beautiful dress, a ring—no. Fuck the patriarchy! I'm getting a beautiful silver heart necklace. I want you all there. We'll have a nice dinner, I'll say my vows, you'll all witness them, and then we'll celebrate."

"I want to do it too," Missy said.

"Really?" Ally asked, thrilled not to be alone in sologamy.

"I'm in," Lexi declared. "I'm so sick of people asking me why I'm still single."

Sabrina chimed in. "Or telling you you're such a catch and wondering why no guy has picked up on that."

Ally wiggled a little in her excitement. "So we'll all do it?"

"Yes!" her friends chorused.

"You know Hailey's going to see this as a threat," Missy said. "Her entire business is wrapped up in making couples."

Ally slapped the steering wheel. "I'm inviting her. I'm inviting everyone, single or not, to celebrate with us. Omigod, I'm so excited!"

"I like it," Sabrina said in her naturally compassionate counselor tone. "Love yourself first. Great love will surely follow that path."

"Sabrina!" Ally exclaimed. "That's not the goal. It's not love me to love you. It's simply a vow of self-love. That *you* are enough. We're taught that we need the whole marriage thing to be complete and have a good life. It's the ritual forced down our throats. Now we choose our own ritual. It's about empowerment!"

"We can still allow for the possibility of great love though, right?" Sabrina asked. "We can still love someone else, be open to relationships?"

"Of course!" Ally exclaimed. "But it takes the pressure off. It's not a declaration against men. It's a declaration for ourselves."

"And it sets the bar higher," Missy put in. "That should be part of the vow. Never settle in a relationship. Honor myself, honor my life."

Ally hit the accelerator a little harder in her excitement.

"Missy, that is so powerful. Would you write the vows for us?"

"Me?" Missy asked softly.

"Yes," Ally replied. "You're so put together. So clear. Of course we can all add stuff to the vows, make them personal, but it would be wonderful to have a starting place."

"Sure, if you want," Missy said uncertainly.

"We do!" the women exclaimed.

"Hey, that could be our vow at the end," Ally said. "We do."

"No, it has to be *I* do," Sabrina said. "Sologamy not polygamy."

The women laughed.

"I do," Ally said, trying it out, and then slammed on the brakes at a red light. The women jerked in their seatbelts. "Sorry."

"Next time I'm driving," Missy said.

6

———

Ethan was driving home after a Sunday morning breakfast at Garner's when he spotted the blond head of the woman who was never far from his mind standing on the opposite side of the road in a snug pink tank top and black leggings, kicking the tire of an old white Ford Escort.

He made a quick turn around the block and pulled up behind her. They were in Clover Park not far from Peak Fitness, where Charlotte worked. Ally had probably been working out.

He approached just as she threw her hands in the air and marched down the street away from him, high ponytail bouncing in indignation, apparently abandoning the car. "Ally!"

She stopped and turned. "The stupid thing just died on me!"

"C'mere, let me take a look."

She marched back toward him, her breasts bouncing in time with her harsh steps, which he managed to ignore by the time she got close enough to notice his ogling by focusing on her pink cheeks and lush mouth. He had a real thing for that mouth with its plump pinkness.

"It's broken." She jabbed a finger at the car accusingly. "I called Triple A, but apparently I don't have Triple A anymore and I forgot my wallet because I ran out of coffee so no credit card to *get* Triple A."

Triple A wasn't the only way to get a tow, but he let that slide in favor of the more pertinent fact. "You're driving without a license?"

She growled.

"I'm just saying—"

"I rushed out the door and forgot to transfer my wallet to my gym bag!" She planted her hands on her hips. "Did you hear the part about running out of coffee?"

He cocked his head. "So you remembered your phone and keys but not the wallet."

"Argh!" She punched and kicked the air, looking fierce, and his jeans suddenly had a lot less room. Something about a strong woman turned him on. Strong with soft underbelly drew him in. Not many women fit that description. Ally did.

"Kickboxing class?" he guessed.

"Yes." She spoke through her teeth. "I can kick *ass* now. Go ahead, make my shitty morning."

He bit back the smile he knew wouldn't be appreciated. Instead he popped the hood on her car and peered inside. He was no mechanic, but it seemed the thing to do.

Ally stood by his side. "Is it the engine? Please don't let it be the engine. I can't afford a new car."

"What happened?"

"I stopped at a stop sign and it just shut down. Completely quiet."

"And when you tried to start it again?"

"It flatlined. Not even a peep out of it. Stupid car. Ruining my fitness high. Ugh! Last week I worked out and you tried to give me a ticket, and this week my car dies! It's like some sign from the universe that I'm not supposed to get fit!"

He took in her flat stomach and toned legs. "It looks like it's working. Don't give up."

She smoothed her hair, her voice considerably calmer. "Oh. Really?"

"Really."

"Thanks. That means a lot coming from a fitness freak like yourself."

"I prefer fitness god."

She snorted.

He grinned. "I think it's the battery. Let me give her a jump and see if we can get you back on your way." He maneuvered his Jeep around, facing her car, retrieved the jumper cables from the back of his Jeep, told her to get in the car, and set everything up. A few minutes later, he signaled for her to start her car, and it roared to life.

"Woohoo!" she hollered. "Martin is back in business!"

He grinned and unhooked everything, shutting the hood. *Martin.* Everyone knew cars were feminine.

He stopped by the driver's side window. "Let it run for a while. Give the battery time to charge and then get a new battery as soon as possible. There's a place by the Eastman mall—"

"On my way!" She beamed and his heart stuttered. "Thanks so much. I'm adding get savvy about my car to my goal list."

He leaned down. "I could teach you stuff. Maybe later today."

"Thanks, but I'm really busy. After Martin's fixed up, I've got a ton of planning to do for my wedding on Friday."

His stomach dropped. "What do you mean? Who're you marrying?"

She smiled serenely. "Myself. It's called sologamy and it's a real thing."

He straightened, speechless. An actual marriage to herself? Was that legal?

She pursed her lips. "Let me guess, you think it's dumb."

"No, just different." *And so like her.*

"It's a thing," she insisted.

"Okay," he said slowly.

"Well, gotta go. Thanks for the jump start, Sergeant Case."

"Eth. My friends call me Eth."

She gave him a sweet smile. "Keep up the good work, Eth."

Then she drove off, all happy with her single self.

He drove home at a sedate pace, not so happy with his single self.

~

Ethan told himself it wasn't weird for a police officer to show up in a friend's classroom to teach kids about stranger safety. Sure, he usually passed the duty off to a rookie officer, but this was Ally's classroom and they were on good friendly terms. Only two days ago he'd come to her rescue and jump-started her car. He was also curious about her solo wedding and…aw, hell he was hooked. He couldn't stop thinking about her no matter how hard he tried. He peered through the glass window of the closed classroom door, where Ally was enthusiastically explaining some basic addition on a whiteboard. She wore schoolteacher clothes—crisp white button-down shirt with the sleeves rolled up, navy blue skirt that ended just above the knee, and navy blue flats. Not sexy. Shouldn't be, anyway. He must be caught in some kind of Ally-attraction field, because even her geeky outfit on their hike with the socks on the outside of her pants turned him on. He blew out a breath and focused on the kids. About twenty of them, mixed in their attention. Some of them appeared to be listening, some half asleep, and some wiggling around in their seats and whispering to each other. He would've been the kid in the back, throwing spitballs. He knocked on the door.

She went to answer it, her blue eyes widening. "Eth, what're you doing here?"

He warmed at her casual use of Eth. "I'm here to talk about stranger safety, stepping in for Wayne."

She flushed pink. "Well, this is a surprise."

He tipped the end of his cap at her. "I'll do a good job, ma'am."

She shook her head. "Silly. Of course you will. Come in."

He set the plastic bag full of coloring books illustrating today's lesson on her desk, along with his cap, and then joined her in front of the class. The kids stared in awe. He would've too at this age, seeing a real live police officer in uniform complete with handcuffs, nightstick, and gun. They were probably six.

Ally introduced him. "Class, please say hello to Sergeant Case."

"Hello, Sergeant Case," the class chorused dutifully.

"Hello," he said.

"He's here to teach us about stranger safety." She turned to him. "You want me to gather them on the rug, or would you prefer to stand in front of the class?"

"I'll stand."

"Take it away." She retreated behind her desk and smiled encouragingly.

He cleared his throat. "So does everyone know who the safe adults are in their life?" He knew the required speech. He'd done it before when he was a rookie and had reviewed it before coming in.

The kids all shouted answers at once. "Mommy!" "Nana!" "Daddy!"

"Raise your hand," Ally gently reminded them.

They came to order pretty quickly. He was impressed. A gentle reminder would not have been enough for him at this age. He launched into the ten points he was supposed to get across on safe adults, strangers and their various enticements, the best response to a dangerous situation, and made sure not to give them any time for questions or comments. If he didn't barrel straight through to the end, he'd forget something, and he didn't want to read the lessons straight from the coloring book. That was lame. Several hands were in the air, which he studiously ignored.

Finally, he wrapped up with a review of the ten points and what constituted a safe "green light" situation and a dangerous "red light" situation. "Okay, any questions?"

The hands flailed around. Seemed like everyone had a question. He pointed at the girl with two long braids who was practically falling out of her seat in her effort to stretch her hand toward him. "Yes, what's your question?"

"Are you Ms. Bloom's boyfriend?"

He stiffened.

"Gabby!" Ally exclaimed. "Why would you say that?"

Gabby batted her big brown eyes. "He made the sexy eyes at you, Ms. Bloom." The kids giggled and Gabby nodded sagely at her friends. "I heard my parents talking about it before."

Heat crept up his neck. Was he that obvious that even a six-year-old could tell? And, geez, didn't they hear a word he just said? What the hell was he doing here if they weren't learning something important?

Someone started singing, "Cop and Ms. Bloom k-i-s-s-i-n-g!"

"Stop that at once," Ally said sharply. "Sergeant Case is a friend of mine. Now I want to hear good questions on what he taught you. Remember not all strangers are bad. Safe strangers like a police officer or a teacher can help you. Now does everyone remember how to handle a dangerous situation?"

The kids were quiet. He'd said the phrase several times. *No, Go, Yell, Tell.*

He turned to her. "Maybe we could role-play a few situations."

"Sure." She stood and crossed to him.

"Could you help me feed my puppies?" he asked. "They're in my van."

She looked up at him and smiled sweetly. His heart kerthunked. "No!"

"Louder," he told her.

"NO!"

"Now run away."

She did a little jog back to her desk that had the kids giggling. He turned and gave the kids his best intimidating cop stare. They settled down.

"Then it's okay to yell for help even if we're inside or in a quiet place," Ally said. "When you're safe, tell a trusted adult what happened."

"Yeah," he chimed in. "Remember, a stranger adult shouldn't be asking a kid for help."

They did a few more scenarios minus the running away because he didn't want the kids laughing. This was an important lesson. Ally did a fantastic job, really looking like she was thinking about some of the maybe scenarios, like when he said her mom asked him to pick her up. In some weird way he felt like they were connecting, united in a task, the give-and-take of the role play. He soaked in her bright blue eyes, her beautiful smile, the exuberant energy that seemed to radiate from her.

He had to force himself to focus. The kids were getting louder now, shouting, "No!" right along with Ally.

"I think they've got it now," Ally told him.

"Yeah," he said, surprised he didn't want it to end. Normally these assignments were boring to him. "I've got a parting gift for everyone."

The kids all started talking at once, wondering what it was. A boy piped up. "I hope it's a video game."

Damn, was that kid going to be disappointed. Ethan opened the plastic bag and pulled out a stack of coloring books. They were pretty good for a coloring book—super-hero-themed lessons with lots of cool lightning bolts and bold zigzagging words to color in. "No video games. Coloring books."

"I love coloring!" Gabby said.

"This sucks!" a boy in the back with messy brown hair proclaimed.

Ethan took in the boy's belligerent expression, his faded black shirt with a hole in it, his unkempt hair, and felt a stab of recognition. His chest ached and he couldn't get a word out through the tightness in his throat. Ethan was that kid—hand-me-down clothes, no mom to make sure his hair was combed properly, big chip on his shoulder.

"Nate!" Ally exclaimed. "That is not how we respond to a gift. Say thank you to Sergeant Case."

The boy's lip curled. "You're not the boss of me."

"She's your teacher and you'll treat her with respect,"

Ethan barked. Holy shit. That did not just come out of his mouth. He was *not* that asshole authority figure he'd despised as a kid. Was he? He wanted to be one of the good guys.

Ally shook her head at Ethan and walked to the back of the classroom, stopping to talk quietly to Nate.

Ethan ground his teeth, aware he'd stepped into her jurisdiction. She was the boss here, him barking out orders didn't help her authority with the kids. He focused on counting out the right number of coloring books for each row. The kid in front automatically passed them back. He followed with the crayon packs. And then he couldn't help himself, he walked back to where Ally was still with Nate and waited for her to finish up so he could apologize for stepping on her toes.

"I know I'm not your boss," Ally told Nate in a patient, even tone that probably meant she'd already covered that a few times. "I'm your teacher. Draw your boss for me here." She pointed to the blank page on the inside of the cover.

Nate got to work.

Ally turned and met Ethan's eyes.

"Sorry," he mouthed.

"It's okay," she whispered.

They both watched as Nate drew fast and furious. It was a dragon and pretty damn good for a first grader.

"Wonderful," Ally said. "You're really good at drawing. Be sure to color it all in. I can't wait to see your great work."

Nate flushed at the compliment and industriously continued, adding jagged flames.

Ally turned and spoke to the next kid, encouraging them gently. Ethan just stood there, his heart thumping hard, the blood rushing through his veins, everything in him focused on this amazing woman who reached out to the class troublemaker and turned it around—bam! Just like that. No yelling, no berating, no making the kid stand in the corner. Just gentle encouragement. How would his life have been different if he'd had a teacher like her?

He swallowed down a lump of raw emotion, his gaze locked on this incredible woman like no other. And all he wanted was to be close to her. He wanted her in his life more than he wanted his next breath.

She walked toward him and he forced his hands to his sides, fighting the urge to pull her into his arms.

"Thanks so much for stopping by," she said.

"No problem," he forced out over the lump in his throat that just wouldn't go away.

She turned. "Class, Sergeant Case needs to get back to work. Can you say goodbye?"

"Bye, Sergeant Case," the class dutifully droned.

"Bye, everyone." But he didn't want to leave.

Ally smiled up at him, filling his vision with beauty. "I really appreciate you taking the time to visit. Hope you have a great rest of the day."

"You too," he replied gruffly.

She resumed walking up and down the aisles, checking on the kids, and he took the hint and left.

He stopped outside the classroom door and took one last look at Ally; then he gave himself a mental shake for being such a sap and strode out of the building.

7

Ally nearly vibrated with excitement on Friday night as she entered the posh hotel in New York City with her friends to meet up with their movie star friend Claire Jordan. Claire had arranged a limo for them, as usual when they met up, but instead of a Happy Endings Book Club meeting, tonight they'd have their sologamy ceremony. She was quiet as she approached the private executive lounge with her friends, her mind fully focused on what lie ahead. When Ally had shared her sologamy ceremony idea with her friends and invited them all to witness her marrying herself, she'd originally planned a nice dinner at her apartment. But once Claire understood the empowerment message behind it, she declared she planned to marry herself too! As she put it, honoring themselves could only strengthen the bonds of marriage. After that, everyone got on board. It was the most incredible thing. Claire had told them to pack for a slumber party in her huge penthouse suite to extend the celebration.

They stopped at the door of the lounge, where Claire's bodyguard, Frank, a massive Hawaiian man with a shaved head and a don't-fuck-with-me expression, stood guard.

"Hi, Frank!" Ally said cheerfully. The man never smiled, but Ally knew he was good to Claire, keeping her safe while being respectful of her privacy.

"Ally," Frank responded and opened the door. "Ladies."

She stepped inside and gasped. "Oh, Claire!"

The normally sedate lounge, done in muted grays with white sofas and chairs, had been transformed into a wedding wonderland. She stepped through a wedding arch draped in sheer gauze with fragrant white, pink, and red roses. White votive candles glowed on every surface—the small black end tables, the longer black table now prominently placed in the center of the room, and on the sleek black bar top. White and pale pink flower arrangements stood at the center of each table, and classical music played in the background, piped through speakers in the ceiling.

Claire beamed, her arms outstretched. "You like?" Her usually blond shoulder-length hair was dyed brown for her part as Mia in *Fierce Loving*, making her hazel eyes look more brown than green. Her outfit was elegant and sophisticated—a V-neck black and white striped top with white crystals studded along the V, tailored black pants, and black open-toed heels that were definitely designer. Her closet was designer heaven.

"I love it!" Ally exclaimed, dropping her duffel and sleeping bag and rushing forward to hug Claire.

Claire gave her a squeeze and pulled back to look at her. "I missed you, lady! I was so bummed I had to miss last week's meeting. I love your dress!"

It was Ally's version of a modern wedding gown—an off-the-shoulder white eyelet dress that ended mid-thigh with white ballet flats complete with satin straps that wound around her ankles. She'd skipped the veil.

"Thanks! I love your outfit too."

Claire smiled. "I wanted something more sedate to keep the focus on my personal vows."

Their friends gathered around Claire, who exclaimed over each of them, admiring their dresses. They all had a version of a white dress, mostly sundresses and maxi dresses, except for Mad, tomboy all the way, who had a white pants suit.

"Go ahead and set your stuff by the back door," Claire

said. The rear exit of the lounge led directly to a private elevator.

Everyone dropped off their stuff. Ally removed the manila folder with copies of the vows she'd prepared with Missy's help from her duffel bag and rejoined her friends now gathered near the large center table.

Hailey let out a low whistle. "Did you do all this yourself, Claire? I'm so impressed."

Claire waved airily. "I told my assistant that my friend wanted to get married here in a private ceremony. All credit to Arianna. I'm going to miss her something fierce when she goes on maternity leave. Should we begin?"

The women chorused their agreement and took seats around the table.

"Ally, you sit at the head of the table since this was your idea," Claire said. "You lead us."

"Happy to."

"I'll get the champagne," Claire said. "It's chilling. And we're due to have the food delivered in an hour. It's from the most amazing restaurant. Jake and I had our first date there as real Jake and real Claire." Everyone laughed. It was a crazy story when the two of them had first met, each in disguise as someone else. At least it all worked out. Jake and Claire were happily married.

"I'll help," Hailey said, hurrying to join Claire.

A few moments later, Claire popped her head up from behind the bar, two champagne bottles in hand. Probably the good stuff too. "I got tapas warming back here to hold us over until the food arrives."

Ally couldn't help her wide smile. "You really thought of everything. Thank you so much for making this such a special night."

Claire walked gracefully in her heels to deposit the champagne bottles in the center of the table next to a flower arrangement of pale pink and white roses. Hailey followed, balancing a tray of champagne glasses.

"I'm telling you, this magic is all Arianna," Claire insisted. "She's a wizard with the details. Anyone know someone who'd like to be my assistant, let me know. There's a ton of organizational details to see to, but I promise I'm a good boss. And of course there's perks, award shows on occasion, black-tie events."

"I might be interested," Ally blurted. It sounded kind of glam and she adored Claire. It might be just the thing for her next adventure. She'd been feeling restless in the classroom lately, even though she loved the kids.

"Awesome," Claire said. "Let's chat later."

Ally nodded once, a calm settling over her, like her entire life was finally falling into place. She handed out the vows. "I thought we'd go around one by one, say our vow, and then everyone could congratulate that person, and then the next one goes. At the end, we'll all toast together. Unless you wrote your own vow, then of course feel free to say that one."

The women exchanged glances.

"Nobody wrote their own vow?" Ally asked.

"Yours looks wonderful," Carrie said.

"Good with me," someone else said. The women all murmured agreement.

Ally took her seat. "Okay, let's take a moment of silence to center ourselves. Close your eyes, deep breath in and out." Ally had barely finished with the exhale when Hailey startled her with a sharp, "Ladies!"

Hailey stood, beautiful as always in a white lace cutout dress with exposed holes on her sides, the dress ending just past her ass. "I have a confession."

The room went utterly still.

Hailey smoothed her long strawberry blond hair. Her pale blue eyes held an abject expression of guilt. "I haven't been walking my talk. I've worked so hard to plan happy endings for other people all while keeping myself closed off from the possibility of the same for myself." She bit her lip, apparently waiting for them to condemn her. Not likely.

"We all know that," Mad said bluntly. "Otherwise you'd be hooking up with Josh by now." Only Mad would have the nerve to say what they were all thinking. Mad was Hailey's closest friend despite the fact they were, on the surface anyway, so different. Hailey, a poised beauty queen, feminine to her core, and Mad, a tough blackbelt with gruff manners and a die-hard tomboy.

The women quietly agreed on the Josh assessment.

"Would you please just let me finish my confession?" Hailey asked Mad. "This has nothing to do with that scoundrel of a brother of yours."

Mad snickered.

Hailey went on. "Anyway, committing to myself in this way has made me realize it's time to honor myself and line up my life's work with my actual life." She paused dramatically and took a deep breath. "I've had a friends-with-benefits situation for years, which I just ended. Right before I came here, actually." Her eyes were wide and beseeching. "I know you must think I'm a total hypocrite being a happy ending facilitator—"

"Who's the guy?" Ally interrupted, thrilled to hear the real deal. They'd all been wondering about Hailey for years. It was so odd how she acted like a relationship expert yet never mentioned any guy in her life ever.

"How come we never saw him?" Mad asked. "Is this one of those fake boyfriends?" She widened her brown eyes. "Sure, your boyfriend from Canada who we never see. Ri-i-i-ght."

Hailey huffed. "He's not from Canada. He's my friend from college. We've always just sort of gotten together whenever, you know, casually. He lives in DC, and when he's in New York on business, if he's not seeing anyone, and I'm not seeing anyone—"

"Which you never are," Mad put in.

Hailey ignored that. "Then I meet up with him at his hotel in the city. Liam's a nice guy, well mannered, cultured."

Missy got right to the point. "The sex must've been fantastic if this went on for years. Got a picture?"

Hailey whipped out her phone and showed Missy his picture.

"My God," Missy breathed, "he looks like a model."

"Gimme," Mad said. The phone got passed around the table.

Ally finally got to check it out. She looked from the handsome strawberry blond Liam to the beautiful strawberry blond Hailey. "He actually looks a lot like you."

Hailey walked over and took her phone back, staring at it. "I guess we do have similar coloring."

"He's the male version of you," Ally said. "Right down to the high cheekbones."

Sabrina grabbed the phone and stared at the picture.

"Maybe that's why we were compatible," Hailey said.

Sabrina looked up. "Do you think he's your secret brother?"

Hailey snatched her phone back. "Omigod, no! I'm an only child. My dad died when I was three."

"What if he had kids you don't know about?" Sabrina asked gently.

"He's not my brother!" Hailey exclaimed. "We're the same age."

"Same birthday?" Mad asked and, at Hailey's fierce glare, added, "What? Twins happen."

"No," Hailey said. "Different birthdays. I've met his parents. He looks like them. It's a coincidence." She crossed to her seat and flopped down. "I think we're getting off topic. I just wanted to share that I'm fully committing to our sologamy ceremony."

Not good enough for Mad. "If he's nice and the sex is good, how come you never got together with him?"

Hailey frowned. "I don't know why we never fell in love. He wanted me. But unlike most guys, he was up front about why and that he only ever wanted casual."

"What was his reason?" Ally asked. "I mean for why he wanted you."

"Duh, sex," Mad said.

"He liked my looks," Hailey said in a small voice. And then louder, "Which at least was honest. I was tired of guys hitting on me only to be interested in the surface, leading me on like there might be more."

"Oh, Hailey," Claire said sympathetically, "I completely understand. Before Jake, men used me for what I could do for them in the industry, but you're so much more than the package. I'm so glad you're not going to settle anymore. You deserve more."

Everyone chimed in their agreement.

Hailey wiped away a tear. "Thanks, ladies. I told myself the arrangement with Liam was ideal, but now I see it was a way of holding myself back. I always knew he'd be around. He's been around for years now."

"Maybe he's in love with you," Ally said. She couldn't imagine why else a guy would be available off and on for years. Unless the sex was off the charts. Hmmm…

"He's not," Hailey said tightly. "When I ended it, he said that was okay because he recently met someone and he thought it might go somewhere." She pasted on her beauty-queen smile and Ally instantly knew her friend was hurting. They all did, everyone giving her sympathetic looks.

"So no hard feelings," Hailey choked out and then broke down in gut-wrenching sobs.

The women quickly gathered around, rubbing her back and murmuring sympathies.

"Did you love him?" Ally asked gently once Hailey had quieted again and everyone had returned to their seats in somber silence. Ally was all too familiar with the big buildup and devastating disappointment of unrequited love.

"No!" Hailey dug a tissue out of her purse and carefully wiped under her eyes. Her mascara was apparently tear-proof. "I guess I just thought maybe someday the thing with Liam would go somewhere, you know, when the time was right. I know that sounds dumb. It would've happened by now, right?" She squared her shoulders and took a deep breath. "I didn't mind the casual nature of our relationship because it made it so easy for me to focus on building my business. I desperately needed that solid foundation, for me, you know? You have no idea how unstable things were growing up, but now I'm going to be in *Bride Special*. When that comes out next August with Carrie's wedding in it, I'm set. There's nothing better for national publicity." Hailey had been lucky enough to score a feature article as a wedding planner extraordinaire in *Bride Special*. In a cool turn of events, the magazine people had witnessed Zach proposing to Carrie and had invited them to be the featured wedding in conjunction with Hailey's spotlight.

Hailey took them all in. "Tonight with full honesty and commitment, I enter into these vows. To honor myself and my company's mission. And to be open to future relationships."

Stunned silence.

"Wow," Missy said. "That was a good vow."

Hailey let out a sniffly laugh. "I'm sure what you and Ally prepared is even better. Ally, would you like to lead us now?"

"Absolutely," Ally said, rising from her chair. She looked around the table at the women who were like sisters to her, faithful companions on this great journey, and began. "On this most special night, surrounded by friends who love me, I vow to love myself.

"I vow to take care of myself,

"to seek out fulfilling work and purpose,

"to live my dreams,

"to accept my flaws unconditionally,

"to forgive myself,

"to know that I am worthy of love,

"and to treat myself and others with love and respect."

She took a moment to soak in the significance of the words, tears pricking her eyes at the commitment she should've made to herself long ago. She pulled a jewelry box from her purse and removed a sterling silver heart necklace and held it up with a smile. "With this beautiful reminder of self-love, I do." She put it on and rested her hand on the heart.

The women applauded and whistled. "Congratulations, Ally!" they chorused.

She sniffled, more moved than she thought possible. "Thank you," she managed over the lump in her throat. She plunked down in her seat.

Sabrina, sitting next to her, clasped her hand warmly. "That was beautiful."

"Thanks," she whispered.

"I'll go next," Sabrina announced. "I brought my grand-mother's emerald ring for my symbol." She set it in front of her, stood, and held up a hand with a short laugh. "I'm shaking."

The women encouraged her. Sabrina didn't often speak in front of the group. She was on the shy side, more comfortable one-on-one. Finally, she launched into the vows with a quavering but determined voice.

Ally got choked up. Everyone did. It was powerful stuff.

With each of her friends' vows, the love in the room grew. A palpable force. The strength of the women, their determination to support each other and themselves. It was perfection.

They finished with a champagne toast. "To us!" Ally declared and they drank.

"Let's eat!" Mad exclaimed.

Everyone laughed.

"Before you all snarf down the tapas," Claire said, "the honeymoon starts tomorrow. I made you all appointments for the hotel spa. Massages, facials, mani-pedis, the full deal. In honor of you!"

"Thank you, Claire!" Ally exclaimed and rushed over to hug her.

Pretty soon they were in a massive group hug, laughing and exclaiming, bonded for life in the most important commitment of all—to themselves.

A short while later after champagne and tapas, they sat down to a delicious dinner they passed around family style. Filet mignon, grilled salmon, vegetable lasagna, and all sorts of sides—cauliflower au gratin, brandied mashed sweet pota-toes, green beans with almond slivers. And then the best part —a huge ten-layer tiered wedding cake with pink roses. On the top was a pink heart where the bride and groom would be. Pink for female solidarity.

Ally floated on a happy cloud, surrounded by her sisters.

They all went to Claire's penthouse suite afterward—a

massive suite of rooms that took up the entire top floor of the hotel. The place was decorated in shades of white and silver with royal blue accents with two bedrooms, a living room with a big-screen TV, a dining room with seating for eight, and a kitchenette. They dumped their bags in the living room and headed to Claire's bedroom with its walk-in closet for their favorite game—try on Claire's designer clothes in a fashion show. Claire was so generous she frequently sent them home with a favorite item.

After that, they settled into the massive living room, sitting on the long sofa or on the floor, talking, talking, talking.

Pregnant Charlotte yawned and that immediately set the women into action, getting ready for bed. They all took care of Charlotte, mindful of her pregnancy. They settled into sleeping bags with Charlotte on the sofa to make it easier on her back.

Lights out and the talking continued. The best time for talking, when the secrets came out.

Charlotte had been warned she might be put on bed rest soon. Her pregnancy was considered high risk because of previous severe endometriosis. That had given them all a scare, but then Charlotte insisted they keep positive.

Sabrina had been spending time with Logan Campbell, strictly as friends. Apparently, he'd recently rented office space in the same building where she had her counseling practice. Though, of course, they all called her on it. If they were just friends, why had she kept it secret? Her reasoning that she didn't want people to make a big thing about it had them settling down, not wanting to be the one she referred to as making a big thing.

Hailey worried things were going too well with work and the other shoe was going to drop at any moment and she'd be back to square one. They all assured her she was already a huge success.

Ally shared that the sologamy ceremony was the crowning moment of glory for her new single me, happy me plan.

Missy confessed she didn't believe in lasting love, which was why she was so happy they all did this sologamy ceremony. She could never divorce herself.

Each secret led to much speculation and advice. Exactly what good friends were for. After a while, the conversation trickled down to a few whispers as her friends fell asleep.

Ally curled up on her side and closed her eyes, facing Carrie, Sabrina on her other side. Ethan's sexy smirk came to mind. Now that she knew he was single, she could lust guilt-free. The more she saw him, the stronger the attraction. But where was his head at? Was he messing with her? Did he want to mess around with her?

She got a heat flash just thinking about it. No, no, no. She was not going to spend her solo wedding night thinking about Ethan's well-formed body or his gorgeous face or his smirky dirty sense of humor. She sighed. It had been an embarrassingly long time for her. Dean, then Mark, she did some quick mental arithmetic and realized the number was in the vicinity of…oh, man, way longer than a year. She couldn't bear to dwell on the actual number.

That got her thinking of Hailey's friends-with-benefits situation and how it had kept Hailey single for so long because she had the sex part taken care of and it left her plenty of time to focus on her wedding planning business.

Could Ethan be her friend with benefits?

Carrie poked her arm. "You awake?" she whispered.

Oh, thank God. A distraction. That was a dangerous line of thinking. "Yes," Ally whispered back.

"Will you be my maid of honor?" Carrie asked.

Ally's eyes teared up. "Of course, I'd be honored." She went to squeeze Carrie's hand at the same time as Carrie reached out and they smacked hands and then squeezed. "I've missed our talks."

"Me too," Carrie whispered. "We should have some more girls' nights out, especially with so many of us busy with our guys now."

"I'd like that. What did Zach say about you marrying

yourself?" That was her fiancé, a professor of anthropology, who cooked amazing meals.

"He thought it was fascinating. He did a bunch of research and told me it's a growing trend here and internationally."

"Such an academic."

"He is," Carrie said dreamily.

"Hard to believe you once thought he was a bad boy."

"He still is in the bedroom."

Ally didn't want to hear it. Her own sex life sucked. "You think friends with benefits ever works out? Like you just stay friends with that person even if you stop the benefits part?"

"Ooh, boy. I think it would get real complicated real fast. It's not easy to separate sex from emotion, especially for us. You're a lot like me, happiest with a long monogamous relationship."

She sighed. "You're right."

"Who's the guy?"

"I don't want to say because then you'll look at him funny."

"Ethan?"

"How did you know?"

Carrie giggled. "I saw you guys at Garner's after book club. You had a brief chat and his eyes followed you everywhere. He's a great guy. Zach considers him a brother since they grew up in the same foster home. If you married him, then we'd be even more like sisters."

Ally's jaw clenched. It was like Carrie completely missed the whole point of tonight's ceremony. "I'm on this new empowerment path," she said patiently. "I'm trying to find my own happiness."

"Hey, you're talking to the queen of empowerment. Remember my crazy plan to meet a bad boy and get sexually liberated? New clothes, new contacts, new attitude, even new career path. But guess what? With the right guy, you can still be empowered. Hell, I feel even more empowered now that I'm with Zach. He's so supportive. A true partner."

"Not every guy is Zach," she said, trying to keep the twinge of jealousy from her voice.

Carrie yawned. "Sometimes it's worth the risk of finding out."

Ally fake yawned. "Mmm…goodnight."

"Night, roomie."

Ally's throat tightened. They used to be roommates and had been very close. Ally was still getting used to living alone since Carrie had moved in with Zach. "Night, roomie."

8

———————

Ally woke early Sunday morning back in her own bed, completely rejuvenated from a weekend with friends and a decadent day at the spa. Of course they loved Claire for herself, not her gobs of money, but sometimes it was nice to enjoy it with her. None of them could ever have afforded a spa like that on their own. Before they'd headed home last night, Claire assured Ally the assistant job would be hers if she wanted it, but she wanted Ally to first talk to her assistant, Arianna, to get an understanding of exactly what it was like because, as Claire said, "It's not always glam. Some- times it's like wrestling an octopus trying to keep on top of everything." Ally promised to talk to Arianna and think it over before moving forward. Claire wasn't in a rush since Arianna wasn't leaving for a couple of months when *Fierce Loving* wrapped just before Thanksgiving. Claire was taking off for the holidays. After the New Year was soon enough and would give Ally's boss plenty of time to find a substitute.

Ally was giddy at the idea of working in Hollywood. It certainly wouldn't be boring. And she'd probably get to travel. Claire was always moving with the location of her current movie.

She smiled to herself, loving this newfound contentment in knowing *she* was enough. She didn't have to hope and wish that a prince would show up and give her some fantasy happy-ever-after. She had the happy-ever-after already, mostly. Great things were happening. She sat up and snagged her phone from the nightstand, eager to text her friends congratulations messages on their newly solo married status.

As soon as the phone powered on, she found a text from Ethan. *Hike today at one. You up for it? There's a cave. Intermediate level.*

A cave? Who could resist a cave? Even though it had been a tough haul on the last hike, she'd been proud of herself for finishing it. After two weeks of doing the daily exercises Charlotte had given her, she was already feeling stronger and more fit. It was the first weekend of October, her absolute favorite time of year, crisp and cool, the leaves bursting with color. And a group hike felt safe. No chance she'd climb his incredible body surrounded by other hikers. She quickly texted back. *Yes.*

He responded immediately. *You want to get a bite to eat before?*

Super casual lunch between friends? No prob. *Sure.*

I'll pick you up at 11:45.

She texted a smiley emoticon that he didn't respond to and quickly switched over to a group text congratulating her friends. Tons of confetti, champagne, and dancing emoticons texted back to her. She let out a small happy laugh.

She hopped in the shower and found her mind wandering to shirtless Ethan on their last hike. *No, you are not obsessing over a guy.* She worked the shampoo into her hair and made herself focus on the wonderful weekend she'd had with her friends.

He'd given her the shirt off his back.

That meant something to her. It spoke to his nature— protective, chivalrous, generous. She'd have to be made of stone not to notice his masculine beauty, bronzed skin and sculpted muscle. No scars or tattoos either, just smooth skin that she longed to touch and kiss and taste. She sighed dreamily and then groaned. She would *not* be falling head over ass in lust again. She always spent too much time thinking about guys. Thinking, not doing.

She quickly finished up in the shower. She wouldn't try to look nice for him. She pulled on another tick-repellant outfit —an old thin white sweater, khakis, and tube socks on top of her pants. She stared at the socks and quickly tucked them back under her pants. No makeup, and she tied her hair back in a simple ponytail at the nape of her neck. She stared at herself in the mirror. Her skin glowed from the rejuvenating facial at the spa, but that couldn't be helped. She pulled out the hair band and shook her hair out.

Nerves skittered through her, and she took off the entire outfit. It was too early. She'd do her workout routine, relax with a book, and then get dressed at the last minute because this was just a casual outing between friends. This wasn't a date. She'd gotten off track for a minute there. Now she was back.

By eleven thirty, she'd accomplished a lot—worked out and read five pages of the romantic second-chance story from book club before her high energy level forced her to put the e-reader down and clean her apartment. She dabbed the sweat from her face with a tissue. Shower? Nah. She'd just get sweaty again on the hike. She got dressed in her tick-repelling clothes, grabbed her sun hat and purse, and headed out the door. She got all the way to her car and halted unsteadily. She wasn't driving; Ethan was picking her up. Her stomach did a jittery dance.

Okay, calm the fuck down. Her shoulders sank, disappointed in herself for getting so worked up over seeing him when she'd tried so hard not to be. She had to let go of all this guy angst and steady herself. That sologamy ceremony meant something. Oh! She'd forgotten her silver heart necklace. That would be a good reminder.

She turned, heading for the stairs when she ran into Ethan. "Hey! You're early!"

He gave her a slow sexy smile that made her stomach dip and her pulse thrum. His dark blue eyes ate her up, lingering on her lips, drifting to her neck, and then a slow perusal down her body. Her breath hitched. Finally his eyes locked with hers. Hungry and hot.

She gulped.

"I made better time than I thought," he said gruffly. "Ready to go?"

"Just need to grab one thing." She headed for the stairs and he followed. She glanced over at his gorgeous profile, sharp cheekbones, just a hint of scruff on his square jaw. Deliciously rugged good looks. She quickly faced forward. "Oh, you're coming with, well, okay, sure, I wouldn't leave a friend out in the cold." Not that it was cold. It was freaking hot whenever he got close.

He stopped. "I can wait here if you're not comfortable."

"Don't be silly. No big." She picked up the pace, anxious energy driving her. "So what's the deal with this cave? Is it really old?"

"It's been there a long time, don't know exactly how long. Legend is the Furman lived there all winter."

"The Furman? You mean like a trapper?"

"Yeah. But he was kind of a wanderer. He traveled all over the Northeast, trading furs, but he wintered in that cave. They called him the Furman not just because he sold furs, but because he wore a huge fur coat made up of all kinds of animal furs stitched together. This was back in Civil War times. They say he never spoke."

"That is cool!"

He flashed a smile that made her pulse skyrocket. "It might just be a legend. There weren't good written records back then. Though there is an old picture of him at the Trailside Museum."

"Ooh!" She grabbed his arm impulsively, met hard warm muscle, and quickly dropped her hold. "I've got to see that."

"Sure thing. After the hike." He grinned. "Got to give you some motivation."

"Ha! I'm going to own that trail."

"Own it, huh? Nice."

They reached the top of the stairs and she opened the door to her apartment. He followed close behind, looking around curiously. "I haven't had time to do much decorating," she said.

"It's nice."

"I like more color. I'll probably paint the walls a deep gold. Be right back!" She headed to her tall chest of drawers, where she'd left the necklace in the narrow top drawer, and slipped it on. She closed her eyes, deep breathing as she held the heart, rubbing her finger over the rounded surface, bringing back the contented feeling when she'd put it on at the ceremony. She opened her eyes, centered again, and headed back to the living room.

Ethan was standing in the center of the room, arms crossed. He wore a simple gray T-shirt and faded jeans, but still held an air of authority. In fact, when he wasn't smiling, he made an imposing figure, sort of filling up the space with barely restrained masculine power. Not just strength, but a tightly coiled energy. Like a grizzled outlaw in the Old West. She was glad he was on her side.

"Ready," she chirped.

He immediately headed for the door and opened it for her. "I got you tick repellant."

She halted in front of him. "You got me tick repellant?"

"It was highly rated. Works for twelve hours."

Her heart squeezed at this kindness, a warm glow spreading through her. He wasn't expressive, but then he did this kind of gesture, knowing her concern about ticks. "Thank you, Eth. I really appreciate it."

His lips parted in surprise. "No problem." His tone was brusque like he was embarrassed by her appreciation.

She locked up and they headed downstairs.

"So what'd you have to get?" he asked.

She lifted her heart necklace from under her shirt. "My commitment necklace. I married myself on Friday with all of my friends. They got married too."

"Huh."

Normally she would find that kind of remark offensive, a noncommittal "huh" in the face of such significance, but now she was a new woman, accepting of her flaws and those of others. Like men who couldn't string together enough words for an adequate response to important news.

She tucked her necklace back under her shirt and patted it. They reached the bottom of the stairs and he gestured toward his Jeep. Then he held the passenger door open for her. She climbed in, already used to him doing the gentleman thing. She was sure it was Mr. Campbell's influence. All the Campbell men had been raised with excellent gentleman manners and Ethan had grown up close to them.

She waited for him to close the door. Instead he just stared at her, his brows crinkling together like he was thinking hard.

"So even Claire and Charlotte got married?" he asked. Those two were already married to their husbands.

She laughed. "Yes. It's not a legally binding ceremony. It's a commitment to self, to love, honor, and cherish. To accept my flaws, to be kind to myself. We even went on a honeymoon."

He smirked.

She wagged her finger at him. "I know what you're thinking with that smirk, but it was actually a beautiful thing. We all stayed in Claire's penthouse suite and spent the whole day Saturday being pampered at the hotel spa. I feel like a new woman."

His gaze dropped to her mouth. He met her eyes, his expression unreadable. "Congratulations to you and yourself. Top down or up?"

"Thank you! It's good up."

He shut the door and got in the driver's side. She was suddenly hyperaware of him in the close confines of the Jeep. His woodsy male scent, his large hand on the gear shift, his strong profile, his utter composure. There was a stillness on the surface of him that made her want to find out what was underneath. Did he ever let go? Did he have moments of excitement?

And why did it matter?

She gave herself a mental head shake.

He pulled out of the lot. "Pizza okay?"

"Sure." She stared out the window, barely seeing the

passing scenery—trees in a blur of fall colors—while her thoughts jumped all over the place. Sexy Ethan. Her spectacular relationship face-plants. The painful aftermath. The sologamy ceremony. Exactly how long did she need to commit to herself before letting a man into her life? Six months? A year?

Could she take the edge off this lust with a friends-with-benefits situation? It didn't have to be a big thing, right? It wouldn't be jumping in with both feet if she just tiptoed into this one small part of being with a guy.

"I'm glad you could make it today," he said gruffly.

She turned to him and worked hard to sound normal—not like a sex-addled woman on the verge. "Me too. This fitness stuff is really starting to work for me. Like I actually look forward to it and feel better afterward."

"That's kind of the point."

"Okay, Mr. Muscles."

He flashed a rare big smile. Her breath caught, her heart hammering. Oh, this was bad, bad, bad. He had way too big an effect on her.

"I thought I was Mr. Tough Guy," he said.

She tore her gaze away. "You're both."

His voice was gentle. "Is that good?"

"Only you can answer that." Because she was rapidly melting into a puddle of lust.

He was quiet.

"Did you bring extra weight in your backpack again?" she asked.

"Yeah."

"Mr. Muscles Tough Guy for sure."

He laughed, a short bark of a laugh.

She fingered the silver heart, her skin hot underneath the cool metal.

Ethan tried not to think too hard on Ally's wedding to herself and what it all meant during their lunch, but his mind kept circling back to it. He waited until she had a chance to eat a slice of pizza and was pushing her salad around with a fork before saying, "So how did Claire get married to herself when she's already married to Jake?" *Chicken.* That wasn't the question he really needed to ask.

"I told you it's not a legally binding ceremony." She chomped on a crouton, looking thoughtful. "It's more about honoring yourself. Vowing not to settle for less than you deserve, especially in relationships. Sets the bar higher, you know? I'm learning to be content as a single person. I guess you already figured all that out, but it's new for me."

He wasn't content. He ached with want. Not just lust either. He wanted a home. A *real* home with a family of his own. His blood. Losing his foster mom weeks ago had put that all into perspective. "I guess," he muttered.

Ally set her fork down. "Eth, for the first time in my life, I'm fully content to make my life fantastic all by myself."

He finally spit it out. "So what's the plan now that you've taken this vow? You gonna be single for a long time?"

She stared at the table. "I'm not sure. I'm still figuring things out." She met his eyes, seeming to be searching his expression. "If the right person came along at the right time…"

He held his breath. Was he that right person? Did she see that in him?

She swallowed visibly, looking away. "The point is I'm not spending all my energy looking and hoping and wishing."

"Huh." *So how long do I have to wait before I make a move?*

She wiped her mouth with a napkin. "If by 'huh,' you mean awesome, then I agree."

"Did you used to spend a lot of energy wishing?" He didn't wish for anything. He made it happen or it didn't.

She gave him a small almost sad smile. "Maybe it's not the same for guys. I grew up wanting to be Cinderella and waiting for my prince."

"Yeah, no fun to be waiting around for someone. Better to just live your life and then, if you do meet someone, go for it."

Once you get the signal, he added silently. He needed a signal.

She cocked her head and smiled sunnily. "Now where were you ten years ago?"

The blood rushed through his veins. "Right here working."

She waved airily and then started gathering the trash from their meal. "Not literally. I was sixteen back then. That was the beginning of my romantic fantasies."

He helped her gather the trash. "Tell me your fantasies." He didn't expect an answer. He'd been half teasing anyway.

"That's exactly the point! They weren't my fantasies. They were propaganda." Her voice rose in indignation. "A sparkly glittery fairy tale where I'm passively waiting for the one perfect prince who will take me away from myself and gift me with eternal happiness." She stood and glared down at him still sitting at the table. "You see how that could fuck someone up?"

He stood. "Yes."

"Well, no more. I quit." She marched over to the garbage can and shoved the trash in.

He followed suit. Then she smashed her large hat on top of her head and snarled, "Ready."

"Easy, tiger. I'm not the enemy."

"Sorry, I get really worked up about this. It's not right that women have this stuff fed to them at such a young age. It really fucks with your head."

He placed himself firmly on her side. "Where the hell would you find a prince anyway, right? Unrealistic."

She laughed. "It's not actual royalty. It just means a man who's handsome, strong, spouts poetry, makes you feel like you're the center of his world."

He would do all of that if it meant he could have Ally in his life. He headed for the exit and held the door open for her. "Poetry," he said as she passed, "sounds like a wuss."

She laughed. "Tough guy."

Pace yourself.

Once they were on their way to the reservation, he asked

in a teasing voice, "Think you can keep up with me on this hike?"

"I'm sure gonna try. As long as it's not an uphill climb."

"Uh, didn't I mention the cave's at the top of the mountain?"

"A mountain!"

"Well, more like a large hill. Don't worry. I'll carry you if I have to."

"You will do no such thing."

He found himself smiling again. Couldn't be helped. He dug her fighting spirit. He'd still carry her if she needed a break, though.

Turned out Ally didn't need any assistance. This time she wasn't dead last in their group of hikers, same people as last time, except for one of the Matts. She was definitely stronger than she'd been two weeks ago. She was working with a personal trainer, but most people didn't have the carry through. They went at fitness halfheartedly. Ally was all in. He had a feeling she was like that with most stuff she got into. No wonder she was reluctant to consider a relationship. She probably threw herself into it one hundred percent, and if that wasn't with a guy who appreciated her, it would just lead to a broken heart. He wanted to be that guy who appreciated her. The *right* guy.

He circled back on the trail and walked by her side. She was humming a happy-sounding tune. Last time she'd been so short of breath she could barely speak. "We're almost at the cave," he said. "We'll stop for a break and Rob'll tell everyone the legend. Mostly for your benefit. Most of us heard it last year."

"Awesome." She pushed her sweaty bangs off her forehead and they fell back all rumpled. "You don't have to walk slow to keep me company."

"I already reached the cave and doubled back."

She blew out a breath. "I won't comment on that."

He grinned. "You want to call me something? Mr. Muscles?"

"No, *weenie.*"

He chuckled.

She grinned. "What'd you bring for a snack?"

"Nothing. I figured the pizza would see me through."

"Oh. I brought homemade trail mix."

"You hungry?"

"Not really. I'll probably just throw it at your head for being such a smug hiker." She did a deep-voiced impersonation of him. "*Already doubled back.*"

He barked out a laugh.

They walked in silence for a bit, the group getting farther and farther ahead of them as Ally slowed down on the steeper part of the trail.

"So-o-o," he said, dragging out the word while he geared up for either a great response or a killer shutdown, "now that you're solo married, if a guy asks you out, would you be open to it?"

She took off her hat and fanned herself with it, taking her time answering. He waited, the dread in his gut telling him he was getting the boot. At least he'd managed a stealth date with the lunch and hike. Still, if she wasn't on board for more, he'd have to chalk today and their previous hike up to a friends thing.

Finally she squashed her hat back on her head and said, "Probably not. I'm on a real good kick here. I want to let it build momentum until it's ingrained in my brain. A habit like taking good care of myself takes three weeks to make it stick."

"How long's it been?"

"Two weeks and I feel fantastic!"

"I…" He stopped himself. He could wait a week. He wasn't desperate or anything. Besides, she was spending time with him.

"Yeah?" she asked.

"Nothing."

Finally they reached the cave and settled in with the group, everyone sitting on the hard-packed ground or a few downed logs. Rob told them the Furman legend. Basically what he'd already told Ally with some embellishments like "sometimes on a full moon you can hear his footsteps."

Spooky campfire stuff. After, they went and checked out the cave two at a time. He went with Ally.

"Pretty small cave," she said, peering into the dark space.

"He lived here through long winters too. Harsh conditions. Good thing he was the Furman."

She smirked. "Furry love."

He smirked back. They were meeting on the same dirty wavelength. Excellent.

They walked away, letting the next group take a look. She wagged her finger at him. "You're rubbing off on me."

He smiled widely, enormously pleased about that. There was no reason not to make a plan with her a week from now. It was the three-week mark that she'd said meant she'd be open to a guy asking her out. "You ever been fishing?" he asked casually.

"No."

"We should go. How's next Sunday? Right here at the lake. I have a canoe and an extra fishing rod. It's peaceful."

Her face lit up and his hopes soared. "Then we can cook whatever we catch over a fire for dinner. I've never done that before!"

"It's catch and release only. But I could bring some hot dogs."

"And we could make s'mores!" Her blond bangs bounced in her excitement. "Omigod, this sounds amazing! Let's make it a big party. You invite the guys. I'll invite all my friends. It'll be like a nature party."

He deflated. "The canoe only fits two."

She smacked his arm lightly. "We'll take turns, silly. Or maybe we'll just invite them for the campfire part. Great idea, Eth! I haven't had s'mores in years!"

He bit back a sigh. "Awesome."

9

———

A week later, Ethan decided he had nothing to complain about. Okay, yeah, he had to share Ally with a bunch of other people at their campfire cookout tonight, but right now he had her to himself for the whole afternoon, fishing on the lake. They were the only ones out here besides a few small boats on the far side of the lake. So far she hadn't caught anything and had been unusually quiet. He didn't fill the silence with a lot of unnecessary chatter. That was one of the great things about fishing, just quietly becoming one with nature.

After a while, she looked around and took a deep breath. "This is nice. I can see why you like it. It's almost like meditating."

He nodded.

She kept talking, confiding in him in a way few people did. "I became a teacher because I love kids, but lately my job just feels too confining, you know? I switched from fifth grade to first grade for a change of pace a couple of years ago when the position opened up, but now I think I need a bigger change." She made a sweeping arm gesture, which made her life vest lift. "I want to get *out* of the classroom and *into* the world. I'm thinking about being Claire's assistant. I spoke to her current assistant and it's a lot of work, but also has some great perks. Travel, award shows, VIP rooms so exclusive most people don't even know they exist. Anyway, I'm giving it some serious thought."

His brows furrowed. "Why would you want to be an assistant when you have a college degree?"

"It could be fun."

"More like you'll be chained to your phone, handling her life." Claire spent most of her downtime in California, the rest of it traveling to different movie locations. Ethan was deeply rooted in Eastman, Connecticut. He'd stayed to give back to the community who'd raised him. More importantly, he wasn't far from retiring on a full pension from the years he'd put in on the Eastman PD. All of this pointed to him staying. He tried to think of Ally's job possibility objectively. He could see the appeal of traveling around the world on someone else's dime, the lure of the Hollywood world. And he didn't want Ally to be unhappy, stuck in a job that stifled her, but he also knew their fledgling relationship wouldn't survive long distance.

She smiled sunnily. "Chained to a phone in Paris maybe? Not so bad."

"Do you really want to work for a friend? What if something goes wrong?"

She stared at him. "Geez, Eth, I'm trying to have a quarter-life crisis here and you're ruining it with all your common sense. I'll admit I'm a little worried about having a friend for a boss. Maybe that's why I haven't given her an answer yet. Or maybe I'm just waiting for something better to come along." She sighed. "I don't know. I just...I need to shake things up. I'm ready for the next thing, whatever that is. Maybe I should just grab this opportunity and hope for the best."

He relaxed a little. She was just restless. "What do you really want to do? If you could do anything in the world."

"Hmm...professional dominatrix."

His jaw dropped.

She burst out laughing.

He shook his head. "You got me."

"Yeah, I'm not so into that."

"What're you into?"

"My vibrator." She clapped a hand over her mouth.

He smirked.

"Maybe I should sell sex toys. Or start a sex-toy company with even better vibrators." She lifted a hand. "Made for women by a woman."

"Been a while for you." *And let me help you with that.*

"Now why do you say that?"

"You mentioned it at the diner with Cali. Plus, so far all your ideas involve sex."

She blushed and looked off in the distance over his shoulder.

"Ally." He waited for her to meet his eyes. "Maybe what you're looking for isn't out there, but in here." He tapped his forehead. "And here." He tapped his chest right over his heart.

Her brows scrunched together. "You mean like yoga? Spirituality?"

"Like living a life of purpose. Whatever that means to you."

She stared at him for a long moment before slowly shaking her head. "How'd you get so wise?"

He barked out a laugh. "I ripped that off Joe. He's been like a dad to me. Anyway, he said that when I was struggling over what to do with my life, and it brought everything into focus."

She stared at him as if waiting for him to spout more deep stuff, so he gave her his honest opinion on her sologamy stuff.

"It's good to take the time to work on yourself, but you don't want to trade one extreme for another."

She cocked her head. "What do you mean?"

He treaded carefully. "Like…dropping everything in your life for something new." He'd choked. Dammit. He wanted to say *don't close off the possibility of us just because you're working on improving your life.*

He tried to work up some better words, but they just wouldn't come out. He didn't know where he stood with her, didn't want to back her into a corner, especially didn't want to say something all feelings-like that she wouldn't return, so he just sat there tongue-tied.

Her fishing line jerked and she squealed, standing up in her excitement and peering down in the water.

Never stand in a canoe!

Splash! They both took a dunk in the lake.

Fucking cold. He should've explained about capsizing to her. Canoes were tippy; you had to stay low and centered. They bobbed on the surface in their life jackets. Neither of them wore a swimsuit, just long-sleeved shirts, shorts, and bare feet. Luckily they'd left their valuables locked in his Jeep.

"I think we scared the fish away!" she exclaimed with a laugh.

He shook his head and quickly retrieved the paddles and his rod. Hers was nowhere to be found. Fish probably swam off with it. "Hold these," he said, shoving the paddles and rod at her. "Gimme a moment to right it."

He maneuvered the canoe back upright, went to Ally, got the stuff and tossed it in the canoe. "It's got water in the bottom, but we can still make it back to shore."

"Sorry, Eth. I'm a nature newbie."

"It's fine. See? This is why I made you wear a life jacket." She'd balked at wearing it, saying she was a strong swimmer.

She splashed him playfully. He wound up for the mother of all splashes and soaked her. Not that they weren't already soaked. He grinned because he even got some plant life in there and it looked like a seaweed wig.

"Sea creature!" she hollered, swiping at it. "Get it off!"

"Relax. It's just some dead eel grass."

"Eel!" Her blue eyes widened, her fingers frantic as she tried to untangle it from her hair.

"It's just a plant." He swam up closer and carefully extricated the offending grass. "There." He tossed it away.

She gazed at him, her lips parting.

That was the sign he needed. That look in her eyes. The attraction electric, a force all its own, drawing him in because he knew with absolute certainty it went both ways. He lifted a hand, gently pushing her bangs out of her eyes. And then forced himself to turn away. He'd end up drowning them both the way he wanted her.

"Got to get to shore," he muttered.

He hauled himself into the canoe, careful to stay low and centered, turned and offered her a hand.

"Won't I pull you in?" she asked.

"Nope. I've got you."

She placed her hand in his and he pulled her up. She flopped ungracefully into the canoe and stayed low, like she was afraid to tip it again. He guided her over to the bench seat and took the one across from her.

She shivered. "I didn't even bring a change of clothes."

"Me either. We'll dry. I'll hang up our stuff, get a fire going."

"Oh, really? And in the meantime we just run around in our birthday suits?"

He smirked.

She jutted out her chin, and he stared at it instead of her lush mouth. God, she was sexy. He wanted her naked so bad he could taste it, though he'd planned on being a gentleman and giving her a hoodie from his Jeep to cover up while their clothes dried.

He lowered his voice to a husky tone. "I'll warm you up once we get to shore."

She stared at his mouth, her pink tongue darting out to lick her lips. Kill him now. "Oh," she said in a breathy voice.

He grabbed the paddles and paddled to shore with powerful strokes.

A few moments later, she crossed her arms, hugging herself. "Damn, I'm seriously cold."

"I have a towel and a hoodie in the Jeep. You can dry off and wear the hoodie. It'll probably fit you like a dress."

She eyed him. "What are you, a park ranger? No. Take me back to my apartment, where I will shower the dead eel germs off me, remoisturize, and redress."

He grinned. "So now I'm a park ranger?"

She nodded once. "If the brown felt hat with the drawstring chin strap fits."

He laughed out loud. "Come on, city girl, stay with me on this. Back to your apartment is the wimpy way to go."

"You take that back, tough guy. I hear an implied weenie in there."

"The guys'll be here soon. They're going to show up to an empty party."

"Then you stay here while I drive your Jeep back to my apartment and change."

"With your lead foot?"

She scowled and then her scowl faded as she watched him paddle. She dug the display of strength, he could tell by the flush of pink in her cheeks. She lifted her head, her expression pure desire. "Did you, uh, want me to help paddle?"

He smirked. "Then how would you ogle my muscles?"

Her cheeks dotted with red. Ha. Busted. She turned away, looking at the shoreline, and then turned back to him. "Let's speed this up, muscle man."

He did, loving the nickname. He got them safely to shore, dumping his fishing rod, paddles, and their life vests on the sand before clearing the water from the canoe. Then he stored the canoe in the designated area a short distance away.

When he returned, Ally was doing a little bouncing dance to keep warm.

He took in her goose bumps, her wet hair pressed flatly to her head, her pale lips, her soaked clothes, clingy and see-through, and did the only logical thing—pulled her into his arms and kissed her. Her lips were soft and yielding, exactly as he'd hoped. She wrapped her arms around his neck, pressing against him, igniting carnal need. Scorching hot, tongues tangling, they devoured each other. He gripped her hair, his other hand firmly on her ass, pressing her against him. She moaned softly, threatening to break his control.

He pulled away, both of them breathless.

She stared at him, her fingers touching her lips.

He grabbed her hand. "Come on."

"Don't you need your stuff?"

He stopped, and she gave him a knowing smile. "Blood left your brain, didn't it?" she asked.

He kissed her again, hard and fast. "You've got a smart mouth."

They stared at each other for a long pulse-pounding moment. He wanted that mouth and a lot more of her. Right here, right now. Kissing Ally had only confirmed what he'd known deep down—they fit. On every level.

She let out a shaky breath and looked everywhere but at him. "Okay, um, so let's go to my place first so I can shower and change; then we'll go to yours so you can too."

He stared at that lush mouth he desperately wanted another taste of. If they went to her place and she was naked in the shower—no. He had to do this right. Not in a hot rush before a party. All things considered, he'd have better control if they stayed here, knowing their friends were arriving soon. "We'll stay here," he said firmly. "You can wear my hoodie."

Her eyes flashed. "I'm not showing up to a party looking like a drowned rat. Let's rock-paper-scissors for it."

He bit back a smile, liking that she didn't hesitate to push back. "What is this, first grade?" He lifted a thumb. "Thumb wrestle. And you're not at all ratlike. You look very natural."

She harrumphed. "Natural is not what I'm going for." She joined hands with him and lifted her thumb. "One, two, three, go."

He won in a quick battle, keeping her hand tucked in his. "Looks like you're wearing my hoodie."

"Only because your thumbs are unusually large."

He lifted his thumb and stared at it. "They are?"

She slammed his thumb down. "Ha-ha! I won. Back to my place."

"You cheated. That didn't count."

She grinned cheekily and headed for his Jeep, a little swagger in her step.

"Fine, you win." He grabbed his fishing stuff and caught up with her, telling himself to cool it. He'd keep his distance at her place, make it quick at his place. That way he'd eliminate the window of temptation. After the party was soon enough. Then he could take his time, make it good for her. For now, he'd keep it light.

She sniffed him. "You smell like the lake."

"What's wrong with that?"

She crinkled her nose. "It's kind of fishy."

"How can it be fishy? All your splashing scared the fish away."

"Trust me, we're like walking aquariums."

"Huh."

He drove to her place, keeping up a steady back-and-forth over her city-girl ways and his country-boy ways.

He couldn't stop smiling.

Ally texted Hailey to let her know she and Ethan would be a little late on account of a fishing mishap, but to go ahead and start the party without them. Hailey would spread the word to everyone else. Feeling cozy and warm in Ethan's hoodie, a thick gray sweatshirt that was so big she could sit on it, she was a lot more comfortable on the drive to her place than she was back at the lake. Well, as comfortable as she could be now that she'd crossed the line with Ethan. Her lips tingled at the memory of that incredible kiss, sensual and passionate. That kiss told her Ethan knew exactly what to do with a woman.

And she desperately wanted him to do her.

No other man had ever turned her on so much with just a kiss.

She wanted to trust him. She wanted him. Her body said yes, her brain screamed no, and her heart was not available for comment, locked up in her tight chest.

She blew out a breath. One step at a time.

She glanced over at him in the driver's seat, looking all composed, not shaken up like her. It was just a kiss. No big. Keep it light.

Ethan parked in front of her building, got out, walked around, and opened her door for her.

"Such gentleman manners," she teased. "I heard Mr. Campbell taught all you guys."

"Yes, ma'am."

She laughed and stepped out of the Jeep. He shut the door behind her. "Thank you."

His gaze raked down her body before meeting her eyes with a hungry look that made her throb. "I like you wearing my hoodie."

She flipped the hood up over her head. "This old thing?"

He held her chin. "You look like you're mine."

She shivered, suddenly breathless, her heart pounding in her ears.

He chuckled, a dirty low sound, and guided her upstairs, one large hand on the small of her back. She moved at a quick pace, spurred by adrenaline. *Think practically.* They were both soaking wet, the priority was getting warm and dry before joining their friends at the party. Yes, the party! A built-in deadline for them to work toward. As long as they kept their distance for just a little while more, everything would be fine. She'd ignore the lust that made her limbs heavy and her belly flutter and all of her feel alive.

One step at a time.

She glanced at Ethan in his soaking wet clothes and realized he must be cold. It was mid-October and the temperature was dropping enough to put a nip in the air. He was too tough to admit to being chilly.

As soon as she got inside, she took off his hoodie and handed it to him. "Here, so you can warm up while I shower."

His eyes were hungry, eating her up. "I'm plenty warm."

She tossed the hoodie at him and he caught it one-handed. She grabbed the remote off the coffee table. "You can watch some sports."

He took the remote. "Exactly how long are you planning to take?"

"I'll try to be quick, but I have to deal with my hair, dry it and everything. I'll get you a towel so you can sit on the sofa."

"I'll stand."

She shook her head, went to her bedroom, got a towel from the closet, and returned, offering it to him. He remained arms crossed, standing in front of the TV. At least he was wearing his hoodie.

She put the towel on the sofa and returned to him. "Now you can take a seat."

He cupped the back of her neck and squeezed, gazing into her eyes. "You don't listen very well, do you?"

Her breath hitched, her pulse skittering, nearly light-headed with lust. "I'm being helpful," she whispered.

"Helpful," he echoed with a hint of amusement like he was onto her ways, trying to be all practical instead of throwing herself at him.

She was caught, his big hand on the back of her neck, so close she could feel his breath. "Eth," she whispered.

He closed the distance, his lips brushing over hers, once, twice, filling her with aching need, until he finally took possession.

She lost herself in the intense pleasure. His hand shifted, cupping her jaw, his other hand cupping her ass, pulling her up tight against him, pelvis to pelvis. She was so turned on she felt like she'd explode at the lightest touch. She wanted desperately to get skin on skin, the insistent throbbing between her legs spurring her on. She slid her hands under the back of his shirt, had barely gotten the tamest of back feels in when he broke the kiss, lifted her by the waist and set her away from him.

"I don't understand," she said in a breathy voice, woozy from the sudden loss of him.

"Timing," he said tersely. "Go."

She didn't go. The temptation was too much. She got closer, rising up on tiptoe to whisper, "We can be late for the party."

His hand came up, cradling her jaw, the roughness of his palm so different from the other men she'd dated. His voice was gruff, an edge to it that excited her. "When I finally get you naked, I'm going to need all night." His thumb swept across her bottom lip. "Understand?"

She was a puddle of lust. Not a single brain cell firing. She nodded, beyond speech.

He smirked and dropped his hand, stepping away from her to stand in front of the TV.

She was halfway between elation and frustration when she headed to the shower.

The moment she stepped into the living room, hair dry, wearing a light pink V-neck sweater and jeans, Ethan barked, "Let's go," and went to the front door, holding it open for her.

She snagged her purse and headed for the door, a little surprised at his turn from hot and hungry to terse. "Why're you so cranky all of a sudden?"

"You have no idea how tempting you are."

She flushed with warmth at the compliment. "Thank you." She beamed, a little giddy that she had just as much an effect on him as he did her. She could forgive crankiness brought on by overwhelming lust for her.

He grunted. "Only reason I'm showering is because you said I smelled like an aquarium."

She followed him outside, locked up, and turned to him. "Don't I smell so much better now?"

He headed for the stairs. "No comment."

She kept up, a cheerful lightness in her step. "You can comment. I do, right? See, this was a good idea."

He moved incredibly fast down the stairs. "This was a terrible idea."

Luckily she was wearing her sneakers and hurried down with him. "But I smelled like dead eels before."

"Dead eel grass. Not dead eels."

"And now I smell like shampoo."

She waited for him to notice how nice the honeysuckle shampoo was, but he remained quiet the rest of the way down.

Ethan stopped at his Jeep and opened the door for her. "You smell like sexy woman no matter what."

She blinked, her stomach doing a delicious flip. Before she

could attempt to return the compliment, he did smell like sexy Ethan under the lake smell, he shut her door and went around the other side.

As soon as he got in, she said, "You too."

He started the ignition. "Too late. Getting a shower."

She stifled a laugh.

"This'll take a lot less time than yours did."

"Clearly you're not used to waiting on a woman."

"Nope."

"Get used to it."

He took her hand and gave it a squeeze. "I'd like that a lot."

Her heart clutched. The unexpected tenderness cracked through the haze of lust, making her think of the possibility of more. Her mind raced forward in time; could they have something lasting?

Stop it. Ethan is not your fantasy prince bringing you a happy-ever-after. She was so mad at herself for backsliding. She'd deliberately chosen a new direction for her life. And she was making great progress too, learning to enjoy singlehood, trying new things, searching for what would bring her happiness. The sologamy ceremony had cemented everything, transforming her from a hopeless romantic to a practical, self-respecting single woman. She'd become the butterfly she was always meant to be. Now she had a great job opportunity on the horizon with Claire, possibly taking her far from home. She couldn't start something with Ethan and then leave. That wasn't fair to either of them.

She was quiet on the short drive over to his place in Eastman, her thoughts jumbled, not at all sure what to do with this intense chemistry between her and Ethan. Could she enjoy something casual with him? If they talked about it, sort of set some boundaries to keep it light, maybe it would be okay. Nobody would get hurt.

She followed him to the door of his two-story townhouse, curious about his place. Probably it would have a lot of wood furniture, maybe even a trophy on the wall, like a deer head or a giant fish.

She stepped inside to a sparsely furnished living room with only three things—cushy chocolate brown leather sofa, wood coffee table, and a flat-screen TV mounted on the wall. No end tables. Nothing hung on the walls. It looked like he'd moved in to the standard white walls, beige carpeting that the townhouse came with and left it. She peeked into the kitchen, separated by a half wall on two sides, to find a round gray steel bistro table with two matching chairs. An adjacent dining room was nearly empty except for some barbells on the side. The place was Spartan and she decided it fit the outdoorsy tough Ethan. Though the sofa did look soft and inviting.

"Just you here?" she asked, crossing to the sofa to put some distance between them. Lust addled her brain.

"Yeah. Logan Campbell used to live here too. It's a two bedroom, but ever since he's become a hotshot entrepreneur, he went and bought a house."

"What does a hotshot do?"

He lifted one bulky shoulder up and down. "He runs an online service that does background checks for short-term contractors and personal caregivers. Ben Wright works with him." He jutted out his chin. "I could've got in on it too, it was my work that inspired the idea, but I told them a desk job wasn't for me."

"Ouch."

He stepped closer. "What do you mean ouch?"

"Well, it's just that he and Ben must be doing really well. You could've bought a house too if you were in on it."

He crossed his arms, his tone hard. "I'm a simple man with simple needs. Happy to work my shift, do a good job, relax with a beer, or go fishing on the lake. Doesn't get any better than that."

He was so defensive she should've let it drop. It wasn't like she cared about money, but she'd seen through Claire the fabulous options money could give someone. "What about travel? Have you ever left Connecticut?"

"Sure, I visited Jake out in California before. I'm happy." Jake Campbell had a billion-dollar tech company in California. Now he was only part-time and moved with his wife, Claire, to her movie locations.

"So you're completely one hundred percent content?" It was hard for her to comprehend coming so close to a fabulous opportunity and turning it down.

He frowned. "Not one hundred percent content. Mostly."

She stepped close enough to touch, drawn to his open honesty. "What would make it one hundred percent?"

His expression softened before he lifted his chin in challenge. "What would make it one hundred percent content for you?"

She thought for a moment. "That's what I'm trying to find out. Maybe finding my life's purpose. You found yours though. And you're still not content?"

He was quiet before finally saying, "There're other factors."

She nodded, figuring he meant something really deep. "Like enlightenment."

"Enlightenment, huh?"

She waved a hand airily. "Enlightenment, peacefulness, satisfaction—whatever word you use, it means the same thing."

He smirked.

"Not that!"

He gave her a slow sexy smile that made her insides flip. "You were thinking it too."

"So every time you smirk you're thinking about sex?"

He nodded. "Pretty much."

"That's a lot."

"I'm a guy. It's kind of our thing." He inclined his head toward the sofa. "Go ahead and take a seat while I shower."

She held up a finger. "Hold on, let me get this straight. So while you're busy thinking about sex most of the time, I'm, well, I *used* to be, busy thinking about my prince galloping up on his white horse to whisk me away?"

"I guess. I never knew women thought that until you just said it."

"It's understood."

He lifted a brow in an arch look of disbelief, his eyes dancing with amusement. Then they cracked up.

"Ridiculous!" she exclaimed, shaking her head.

"Completely fucked up."

She got serious. "I'm just glad I saw the light."

He studied her for a moment. "So now that you're off the prince thing, you gonna join me on the dark side?"

"I'm on the path to enlightenment."

He leaned close with a naughty look in his eyes and her heart kicked hard. "Is that another word for orgasm?"

She tried to laugh it off, though her belly was fluttering and the moment the word *orgasm* rolled out in his deep voice she went damp, well, more damp. "Eth! You're ridiculous!"

He smiled and tapped her on the nose. "Be back in *much* less time than it took you to shower."

"Yeah, yeah," she said and headed for the sofa. She grabbed the remote and flopped down. Omigod, this sofa was decadent. She felt swallowed up in a hug.

She turned on the TV and found a rerun of her favorite medical drama. The sound of water running upstairs distracted her, her mind instantly conjuring an image of shirtless Ethan, all hard sculpted muscle and tanned skin. The rest of him was probably amazing, she'd felt his thick hardness when they'd been pressed against each other. She fidgeted, throbbing between the legs, more than throbbing, like a great pulse of rampant need. She looked toward the stairs. What if she just walked upstairs and stepped into the shower?

She turned up the volume on the TV, drowning out the shower.

It felt like only a few minutes had passed when the TV turned off suddenly. Ethan set the remote back on the coffee table, standing directly in front of her. His hair was still wet and he smelled woodsy and clean. Intoxicating. He wore a snug T-shirt and jeans that molded to his frame. The outfit only emphasized his incredible muscular body.

And she wanted to rip it off.

He offered his hand. "We'd better get going." She placed her hand in his and he hauled her out of the clutches of the sofa. He dropped her hand immediately, which stung. Maybe he was having second thoughts about acting on their lust.

She forced herself to keep her hands at her sides.

He crossed to the front door and opened it. "After you."

"Thanks," she murmured.

They were nearly back at the lake before either of them spoke again. "Eth?"

"Yeah."

"Are you having second thoughts?"

"About what?"

"I don't know. The all-night thing, I guess."

"Are you?"

"Kind of."

"Okay."

She let out a breath, not sure if she was more relieved or disappointed. He'd agreed so quickly. It was for the best. Now she didn't have to worry about getting involved when she might be heading out to Hollywood with Claire. And her heart was safe.

"You're worth waiting for," he said.

Her heart literally stopped and then lurched to life, pounding against her rib cage. Not even her fantasy prince could have topped that.

10

———

When she and Ethan arrived back at the lake, all of their friends were already there, except for a few who couldn't make it. Josh Campbell had gotten a fire started in a ring of stones that hadn't been there before. He must be a pro at the outdoors stuff like Ethan. Several people were cooking hot dogs on long metal skewers held over the flames. Others were sitting in beach chairs, drinking beers or holding red Solo cups most likely filled with wine, and chatting. She let out a happy sigh. This was her favorite way of enjoying the outdoors—food and drinks with friends. She just wanted to hug everyone.

"We're here!" she exclaimed. "Sorry to be so late. We fell in the lake and had to get cleaned up."

Everyone laughed.

"How'd you fall in the lake, man?" Josh asked.

"Ally stood up when she got a fish on her line." Ethan mimicked balancing in a rickety canoe. "Tipped us right over." He whistled and gestured in a dive.

"And I didn't even get the fish!" Ally exclaimed. She turned to Ethan as a thought occurred to her. "Where's my rod?"

He smirked and she jabbed a finger of warning at him. He

grabbed her finger and held it, making her flush with heat. "Fish probably swam away with it." He leaned close, lowering his voice to a husky tone that gave her a hot shiver. "I'll get you another rod if you want to try again."

Her mind instantly turned his words dirty. "Yes," she said immediately with no thought at all beyond getting that rod and riding it. Who knew fishing could be foreplay?

Someone let out a low whistle and Ethan dropped her finger. She looked to where the sound had emanated. Both Logan Campbell and Ben Wright were hiding grins behind their lifted bottles of beer.

So-o-o, okay, maybe it wasn't just her that noticed the chemistry between her and Ethan.

"I'm going to get some wine," she told Ethan.

He jerked his chin. She headed over to where Missy, Lexi, and Sabrina were gathered. Missy held up a bottle of chardonnay. "Want some?"

"Yes, please." Ally looked around. "Where're the cups?"

"I'll get you one," Sabrina said, heading to a small folding card table, where plates, cups, and utensils were stacked.

"You and Ethan looked pretty cozy," Missy observed.

Ally smoothed her hair, fighting back her blush. She wasn't ready to talk about whatever this thing was with Ethan. "He taught me how to fish, that's all. I'm trying new stuff, you know that."

"Uh-huh," Missy said and took a sip of wine.

Sabrina returned with a cup and Missy poured in a healthy serving. "What's the deal with Ethan?" Sabrina whispered.

"Nothing," Ally said, her cheeks flushing. "We're friends."

"Friends don't check out friends' asses," Lexi put in.

Ally whirled. Ethan was clinking beer bottles with a couple of the guys. "Shut. Up. He is not."

"She meant before," Sabrina said. "When you turned and came over here to see us."

Ally took a long swallow of wine. "How's the sologamy stuff working out for you ladies? Feeling empowered?"

"You can still get laid, you know," Missy said. "Sex can also be empowering."

"She's right," Lexi put in.

"I'm fine," Ally said through her teeth. If fine meant insane with lust and terrified of falling head over ass again.

Sabrina rubbed Ally's back in her comforting relationship-counselor way. "Of course you're fine, sweetie. Women can go much longer without sex than men."

That didn't make her feel any better. She scowled at Sabrina, who smiled back, a mischievous glint in her eyes.

"How long's it been for you?" Ally asked.

"Never you mind," Sabrina replied primly, still smiling a little as she took a sip of wine. "Come on, let's get ourselves a hot dog."

The women looked at each other and cracked up.

"You guys have dirty minds!" Ally exclaimed.

"Oh, like you didn't know!" Missy said, bumping her shoulder. "You were right there in the gutter with us."

She laughed and headed toward the fire. Josh gestured them to the extra skewers and then held up the hot dog pack. They all chose one, slid it on the skewer, and gathered around the fire, cooking their dinner. Hailey lingered near the lake, gazing out at the setting sun, chatting with Mad.

Josh cooked a hot dog for himself and called over to Mad and Hailey. "You ladies want a hot dog? They're going fast."

"Sure," Mad said, heading over.

Hailey followed and crinkled her nose. "I don't eat hot dogs."

"But you've never had mine," Josh said. "I cook them the right way." He offered his skewer to her. "Here, give my hot dog a try."

Someone snickered. Frenemy explosion in three, two, one…

"It's junk," Hailey replied, closing the distance between them.

"Just taste it," Josh coaxed.

The guys laughed out loud. Someone hollered, "Yeah, give Josh's hot dog a taste."

Hailey's eyes flashed and she glared in the direction of the guys.

Josh rolled his eyes. "I didn't mean that dirty." He held up the hot dog. "Try it."

Hailey crossed her arms and eyed him suspiciously.

Josh bit back a smile. "You'd know if I was talking dirty, princess, trust me."

"And exactly how would I know?"

He gave her a smoldering look, his voice silky. "You'd be feeling it."

Hailey gasped and shooed the hot dog away. "Get that thing away from me. It's bits and pieces of meat no one wanted."

A petite woman appeared in the clearing, drawing everyone's attention except Hailey, who had her back to her. The last rays of the sun illuminated the woman's white off-the-shoulder peasant blouse with white jeans and Birkenstock sandals. Her dark brown hair hung in long neat braids halfway down her back. Her smile gleamed white against her light brown skin. "I brought vegan hot dogs if you'd rather have that." She held up a canvas bag.

Hailey whirled, her eyes nearly bugging out of her head. "Who're you?"

Josh's face lit up. "Hey, you made it." He crossed to the woman, took the bag, and gave her a kiss. "This is Clarissa. Clarissa, this is everyone."

"Hi, everyone," Clarissa said with a small wave.

"Hi, Clarissa," they answered in near unison. Except Hailey, who just stood there with her mouth open.

Ally handed her hot dog skewer to Mad and then went over to introduce herself to Clarissa, curious about her. Clarissa smiled warmly and shook her hand, her whole demeanor mellow and laid-back. She was like the anti-Hailey.

"You new in town?" Ally asked.

"Mmm-hmm," Clarissa said. "Just moved here two weeks ago."

"And what do you do?"

"She's a massage therapist," Josh put in.

Clarissa inclined her head at Josh, giving him a sexy flirty smile before turning back to Ally. "That's a side gig. I teach yoga."

Josh could not have picked a woman more different from the tightly wound Hailey.

"I used to take yoga," Hailey said. Or maybe they weren't that different.

Clarissa gave Hailey's arm a squeeze. "You're welcome to join my class. We have all levels, beginner to advanced." She turned to the group. "All of you are welcome. Josh has my info if you want to give it a go."

A few of her friends murmured thanks. No one would agree to go, though. At least not in front of Hailey, who still looked taken aback by Clarissa's very existence.

"I brought you a Guinness," Josh told Clarissa.

"You remembered," she said warmly.

"Course I did." Josh headed over to a cooler to fetch it.

"He's such a sweetheart," Clarissa said to Hailey.

"Mmm," Hailey said, her lips drawn in a flat line. "Welp. Great to meet you, Clarissa. I'm sure we'll see each other around."

"You—" Before Clarissa could finish her sentence, which was no doubt going to be a warm "you too," Hailey did an about-face and headed straight for Sabrina. Ally couldn't blame her. Just being near Sabrina could have a relaxing effect. It was her relationship-counselor vibe.

Josh reappeared with cans of Guinness for him and Clarissa. How cute.

Ally checked on Hailey, who had her back to the group, talking to Sabrina. She decided she was in good hands and went to retrieve her hot dog from Mad. "Thanks."

"No problem," Mad said, her gaze darting over to Hailey. They were probably all a little worried about how Hailey was taking this. It just didn't seem right. Hailey had finally broken it off with her fuck buddy, opening herself to a real relationship, only to be shot down. Ally and her friends had privately agreed that Hailey's declaration that she was open to dating meant she was open to dating Josh. Seriously,

Hailey and Josh had been frenemies with a strong undercurrent of sexual chemistry for so long. Everyone had been waiting for all that tension to explode into mad passionate love.

Ally stifled a sigh. Suddenly her hot dog was on fire. "Ah!" She lifted it and tried blowing on it, but that just made the flames go higher. The skewer was snatched from her hands, the hot dog thrown to the sand. Ethan kicked sand over it, smothering the flames.

"You rescued me again," she whispered. First during her Dean reunion disaster, then when she was stranded on the side of the road, then from a capsized canoe, and now from dangerous fire. Like a prince. *Oh no!* How was she supposed to get over her prince fantasy when Ethan kept playing the part?

"I'll get you a fresh one." He retrieved a new skewer and hot dog and guided her cooking, telling her exactly how to get the perfect dog. "Not in the flames, near the flames. And don't get distracted by other stuff going on around you. Fire is unforgiving."

She melted like a marshmallow, all warm and gooey at his care.

After she caught up with her friends, everyone filling up on hot dogs and assorted salads, she rejoined Ethan and some of the guys, who were alternating sipping beers with skipping stones across the lake. She was hoping to get the dirt on Josh and Clarissa.

Ethan was on the end of the line of four guys. She whispered in his ear, "How long has Josh been seeing Clarissa?"

Ethan shook his head. "Must be recent. This is the first time I've met her."

"You think it'll last?"

"Probably not," Ethan said.

Logan, standing on Ethan's other side, offered his opinion in a low voice. "None of Josh's women stick." He'd probably know, seeing as how he was Josh's younger brother.

They all looked over at Josh standing a short distance from the campfire. His arm was wrapped around Clarissa's waist, their bodies turned toward each other as Clarissa spoke. Josh looked captivated.

"Guess there's a first time for everything," Ally said.

A short while later, Ethan volunteered to help Josh put the food away for safekeeping. Ally jumped in, gathering the condiments, pasta salad, and a fruit bowl and tucking it into a cooler. She went with Josh and Ethan, both men carrying a cooler back to Josh's car, hoping to get some answers from Josh directly about his new girlfriend. On the walk there, Ethan explained why storing the food in a secure place was important. Now that the sun was down, the food would attract all kinds of wildlife—raccoons, bobcats, coyotes, occasional bears.

"It's good we've got a park ranger in our midst," she teased. Though she was a little freaked at the idea of any of those animals making an appearance, so she stuck close to his side. He was meatier than she was and would make a tastier morsel for a bear.

Ethan turned to her. "At your service, ma'am. You scared?"

"No." His blue eyes seemed dark, almost wild like an animal of the night. "Have you ever seen a bear out here?" she whispered in case the bears heard.

Josh chuckled and went ahead to unlock his car.

"Yeah," Ethan said. "If they're at a distance, you should slowly back away. Don't run. But if they're right up close, you gotta make yourself real big." He put the cooler down and raised his arms up above her head. "And make some noise to scare it away, screaming at the top of your lungs."

"Yeah, that screaming part won't be a problem."

He gave her hair a tug. "I'll protect you."

And the thing was, she totally believed him.

After they put everything in Josh's car, Ethan told Josh, "We'll meet you back there. I'm going to get the s'mores stuff from my car."

"Need some help?" Josh asked cheerfully.

"No," Ethan growled.

Josh laughed.

"Clarissa seems nice," Ally told Josh. "Have you been seeing her long?"

Josh grinned. "Little over a week. She's great." He turned and headed back to the lake.

"Be happy for him," Ethan said after Josh was a distance away. "He deserves to be happy."

She smiled brightly. "Of course." But her loyalty was always to Hailey. Her friend might be a little over the top sometimes in her matchmaking, but it was all with the best of intentions. She had the most generous loving heart once you got to know her.

Ethan opened the back of his Jeep and she peered inside. "I completely forgot you had the dessert stuff," she said. "Did you get the good kind of graham crackers?"

"There's a good kind?"

"Yeah, not the generic kind. The official kind. I forget the name."

He retrieved the bag of dessert stuff out of an insulated cooler and shut the back of the Jeep. She stuck close to his side for bear-safety reasons. He lifted a graham cracker box to show her.

"That's the one!" she exclaimed, pleased he'd gotten the right one. It wasn't often she had s'mores.

He put the box back in the bag and turned toward her, bringing them into an almost embrace. "Good."

They stood there like that, staring into each other's eyes, kissing distance apart.

His voice was husky. "Ally."

She licked her lips. "Eth."

They grabbed for each other at the same time, the bag dropping to the ground, kissing like their lives depended on it. Her fingers clutched his shirt, his hand cupped the back of her neck, his arm banded around her waist. Flames. Fire. Incendiary kisses that scorched her resistance, leaving her in a puddle of need.

Ethan pulled away first, staring at her, hot lust in his eyes.

"We should get the s'mores stuff," she said on a shaky breath. "Josh probably told them we were on our way."

"Yeah." He scooped up the bag.

They headed back to the party in heavy silence, her legs wobbly from the electrifying lust. He overwhelmed her. It both scared her and exhilarated her. God, she was a mess.

When the party finally broke up late that night, Ethan appeared at her side. "Ready?"

She bit her lip, teetering on the edge of *big mistake* and *why the hell not.*

"Ally?"

If he touched her, she would've caved immediately, but he didn't. He just stood there, giving her the space she needed to think rationally. So she did what was probably the right thing to do, though the words sort of clogged in her throat. "Thanks, but I'm going to catch a ride home with Missy and the girls." She cleared her throat. "We live in the same building."

He pulled her away from their friends and behind the privacy of a large pine tree. "Please don't avoid me. I won't kiss you again if you don't want me to." He searched her expression. "Just tell me, okay?"

She shook her head. "It's okay. It was just...let's call it..." She trailed off, no words adequate enough to describe what she was feeling. It was a full moon, maybe that could explain—

"Crazy lust," Ethan supplied for her.

She stared at him. "Yes! Exactly. Crazy. Like my mind just left the building." She walked her fingers away from her head.

He wrapped an arm around her, tipping her into him. His voice was gravelly. "That's the best kind."

She felt herself softening, pressed against his delicious heat, breathing in his woodsy scent and pure Ethan.

He dipped his head slowly, closer and closer.

She stopped breathing.

He waited, his breath a soft caress against her lips.

She let out a shaky sigh.

Then she grabbed his head, kissing him passionately, giving in to what she could no longer resist. His response was immediate, the kind of fiery kiss that left no question where this was going. Intense. Hot. Erotic.

She tore her mouth away, still pressed tight against him, breathing hard. "Eth."

"Yeah," he said, his voice low and rough.

"I'm sharing a fact with you pertinent to this moment on the condition that you do not smirk."

"Got it."

"I believe I'm dangerously close to being a virgin."

He blew out a harsh breath. "No way. What about that guy at the reunion? You said you were with him for four years."

She sighed and played with the hair at the nape of his neck. "Sadly, it has been *mumble* since I've last done the hokeypokey."

He laughed.

She dropped her arms and glared at him. "You said you wouldn't—"

"Hey, that wasn't a smirk." He pulled her tight against him, smiling, his white teeth bright in the relative dark. "Are you telling me it's been *mumble* since you've last been with a man?"

"Yes."

He stroked her hair back from her face. "I might be able to do something about that."

"I thought as much."

He kissed her. "I'm glad you shared that with me."

"Nothing wrong with helping each other out," she said, hoping he'd understand the friends-with-benefits nature of their arrangement. It seemed the safest way to go for both of them. Casual and light. "Has it been a while for you too?"

"Come on." He took her hand in a warm clasp and led her back to where their friends were packing up.

"I'm guessing no?"

He didn't reply for a few minutes as they passed some of the guys, who sent them knowing looks. Finally they reached his Jeep and he opened the passenger-side door for her. "It's been a little less than *mumble* for me. Don't worry, I still remember where all the parts go."

She laughed and climbed into his Jeep.

She swore he broke the speed limit getting back to his place. He denied it all the way inside his townhouse.

But once they made it to his bedroom, all teasing stopped.

11

Ally followed a quiet Ethan upstairs to his bedroom, which was considerably cozier than the rest of his place. A Mission-style king-size bed with a warm natural wood finish dominated the space with a matching dresser and nightstands. The comforter was a deep green. It was almost like he slept in the forest—the furniture like trees, the blanket like moss or rich green grass. Outdoorsy like him.

She turned at the clatter of Ethan emptying his pockets onto the nightstand—keys, wallet, coins. Seemed like he was just going to strip down without bothering with a lot of foreplay. Cool. That was like the easiest signal that this was totally casual.

She kicked off her shoes and lifted her sweater over her head, hanging it over the footboard for later. She heard a sharp intake of breath and then he was next to her, his rough palms spanning her ribs.

"Ally, you are luscious." His voice was gravelly, his gaze locked on her breasts still cradled in her pink satin bra. Her breasts were on the larger side; most men got a kick out of them.

"Thanks."

His hands slowly slid up her ribs, his gaze still glued to her breasts.

She kept her hands to herself because it was starting to feel like foreplay on his end and she needed to make sure they were on the same page. "Eth, before this goes any further, I want to make sure we're clear on the nature of this relationship."

He closed his eyes as if pained and his hands stilled on the sides of her breasts. His voice sounded strained. "You want to talk about the relationship *now*?"

"This isn't a relationship."

"You just said…" He shook his head and dropped his hands. His gaze met hers. "Yes, *it is*. We had three dates."

"We did not."

He retrieved her sweater and handed it to her. "You want to talk, put this on."

"I'm fine."

"I'm not."

She tossed her sweater to the side. "I just want to be clear, that's all. Naked is where this is headed."

He looked to the ceiling, his chest heaving in and out. Then he pinned her with a hard look, not even peeking at her breasts. "Fishing," he barked, holding up a finger. "Two hikes plus lunch that I paid for and snacks that I shared." Another two fingers went up. "That's *three* dates. I picked you up at your place and dropped you off. I gave you the shirt off my back."

She warmed at the memory of his generosity. "You did. I really appreciated it." And she'd kept it too because she'd loved the chivalrous gesture.

His gaze dipped to her cleavage before he jerked his head up. "You think I do that for just anyone?"

Her brows scrunched together. She had thought it was just his generous nature. Also, those so-called dates hadn't made her a nervous wreck. Sure, she'd fussed a little, but not nearly to the level she normally would if she'd known it was an actual date. Not only that, she'd been wearing an unattractive tick-repellant outfit for two of them and looked like a drowned rat on the other after an unexpected dive in the lake. She couldn't believe she'd been dating Ethan all this time without knowing it after she'd committed herself to singlehood!

He pushed a lock of her hair back over her ear. "I get the feeling I wasn't clear enough. No, I don't do that for just anyone. I typically fly solo or go out with the guys. I've never invited a woman to go hiking or fishing with me."

"You let me into your private sanctuary," she whispered as it hit her how special his dates really were. And she'd not been quiet in his peaceful sanctuary at all.

He didn't respond; instead his hand went to her bare back, slowly sliding up and down, heating her and bringing a delicious shiver.

"I hope I didn't disturb your communing with nature," she said.

"No, you added to it." He cupped her jaw with his free hand, his other hand splayed on her back. "We clear now?"

Her heart fluttered madly. "So this is casual, right?" she blurted. "Like friends with benefits?"

He removed his hands from her body and she immediately felt the loss. "I don't have women friends," he said through his teeth.

She parked a hand on her hip. "What about Cali and Mad?"

"Partner and like a sister. You know I grew up with Mad." His eyes were locked on hers, studiously avoiding her topless state. "Now are we good?"

She wrung her hands together. "Eth, I have a terrible track record with men. I just jump in and—"

"You already told me about your love life. Four years with Dean, quickly engaged to Mark." His eyes were hard and direct. "You've been messing around with the wrong men, that's all."

"But that's just it. I don't mess around. I know I was only with Mark for six weeks, but we were almost married. I'm pretty much a long-term monogamist, and now I'm trying to take things slow, figure out what will make me happy, you know, like you said, find my purpose. I don't want to—"

"I wouldn't call running away from the altar after a six-week relationship a sign of a long-term monogamist."

She narrowed her eyes. "Why do I hear a judgy tone, Mr. Judgy McJudgy Pants."

He flashed a smile before getting serious. "Sorry, it's just that you seem to dive in with gusto, like with this movie star assistant thing, your single me, happy me thing, but with guys, I think you're skittish."

She stiffened. He saw right through her. No one had ever looked that deeply. She let out a shaky breath and sat on the edge of his bed.

He remained standing, solid and strong.

She folded her hands in her lap and stared at them. "I've never told anyone this before, the real reason Dean and I broke up…" She blew out a breath. "It wasn't just because he wasn't ready to settle down. I—" Her voice choked.

The bed creaked as Ethan sat next to her, sliding an arm around her bare shoulders.

She cleared her throat, blinking away the hot sting of tears. God, she didn't want to talk about this, but she needed Ethan to understand why she was such a mess. "I got pregnant."

He let out a harsh breath of air and she barreled on. "This was a year after college. We weren't careful, maybe because we'd been together so long it just seemed inevitable we'd get married one day. I lost the baby two weeks later. He was there for me the entire time, through the fear and shock of pregnancy and through the grief and pain of miscarriage." She swiped at her eyes. "He waited until I finally felt recovered, felt really good about the relationship, like this was a man who would stand by me through thick and thin, and then he pulled the rug out from under me. He dumped me, saying he wasn't ready to settle down."

"And you still wanted to start up with him again?" Ethan asked incredulously.

She glanced at him, sure he was judging her, but too distraught to work up much temper. "I believed him that he wasn't ready to settle down. It was heavy stuff. And I *really* believed in the fantasy of a romantic happy-ever-after. I clung to that fantasy prince idea so hard, waiting and hoping, never moving forward with any man. Except Mark." She lifted her palms. "All I can say is temporary insanity brought on by the pain I was in." Her chin wobbled and she covered her face with her hands. Now he knew her worst secret. Talk about a mood killer.

He pulled her hands off her face and held them. "Ally, I'm not like him. You can trust me. I'll take care with you."

She bit her lip and nodded, appreciating his reassurance even knowing it would never be easy for her to trust and have faith in another man.

Ethan gave her hand a small squeeze. "I'm not gonna mess with your head, or your heart."

She stared at him, speechless at his simple yet expressive words. No man had ever uttered anything like it before. A surge of deep affection turned her to absolute mush and she gave him a tight hug.

He rubbed her back, soothing her, his voice a deep rumble. "No pulling the rug out from under you, I promise." He pulled back and tipped her chin up. "I like you and want to spend time with you."

She blinked back tears, overwhelmed by his sincerity and tenderness. "That means a lot, really, I wish it was that easy for me to really believe."

"Then I'll have to prove it to you."

"No, Eth. You don't have to make up for—"

"Yes, I do."

She hugged him again, snuggling close against his solid chest. "You're so good."

His low chuckle rumbled against her ear. A moment later, he peeled her off him and stood. "Not that good. I'm going to get a cold shower."

"No, wait!" She stood and threw her arms around his neck. "I want you."

"I want you too," he said gruffly.

She glowed under his tender gaze. That he still wanted her even knowing her secret, how screwed up she'd become in her dealings with men, made her feel lighter than she had in years. She slid her hands under his shirt. "Let's not define the relationship. No more heavy stuff, okay?"

He gave her a slow sexy smile before kissing her gently. "My sentiments exactly."

"Are you big on foreplay, or can we just get to it? I'd really like to just get to it."

He barked out a laugh and framed her face with his hands. "No more talking. I need to focus."

"Oh, okay." She yanked down her jeans and panties. "Ready."

He swore and pulled her against him, his fingers tunneling into her hair as he kissed her long and deep. God, she'd missed being with a man and this one was spectacular in every possible way. She stopped thinking altogether. He kissed her for a crazy long time, pulling away just enough to unclasp her bra and toss it before kissing her some more, his hands roaming up her sides, over her shoulders, down her back like he was learning her body by feel instead of sight. He made her melt into a slow burn of need, not rough and hard like Mark or quick and to the point like Dean. Ethan took his time like he wanted to enjoy her.

She wanted to enjoy him too. She yanked at his shirt and he broke the kiss, tearing it off and flinging it to the side.

"You're the luscious one," she said, her hands roaming from his amazing abs with ridges galore on up to his chest and massive bulging shoulders. She lifted her gaze to his eyes burning with raw desire, yet he was so restrained, letting her explore while his hands rested on her waist. That meant so much, like he took care with her just like he said he would. Her eyes stung with unexpected tears and she covered by grabbing his waistband. "Lemme see more luscious."

He stripped out of his jeans and boxer briefs. Her mouth went dry. "Yes," she croaked.

He smiled and then wrapped his arms around her, kissing her and pulling her into the bed, under him.

"Grab a condom," she urged, expecting a hard thrust any moment.

"I will, not yet." He settled between her legs, holding his weight off her with his forearms on either side of her head. He was hard muscle from head to toe, pressing against her softness. He stroked her hair back from her face, sliding his hand down to cradle her jaw. He gazed into her eyes and her breath hitched. Then he kissed her, long deep wet kisses that made her melt into the mattress. She'd never felt so relaxed and so turned on at the same time. Her hands roamed up and down his back, loving the feel of him, solid and strong, his skin hot to the touch.

He shifted to trail kisses down the side of her neck, taking his time, kissing and then running his tongue along the cord of her neck, tasting her. She shivered. He worked his way down, holding her breast cupped in his large hand, lifting it to his mouth, where his tongue flicked rapidly over her nipple.

"Oh!" she cried.

His mouth closed over her breast, pulling her nipple to the roof of his mouth, suckling deep. Her hips lifted of their own accord. Her pulse pounded in her ears, electric sensations racing along her skin, the throbbing between her legs insistent, begging for release.

"Eth, I'm so ready."

He shifted to the other breast, giving it the same lavish attention. Her insides clenched, tight and hot and wet. She was so close already. She cupped his head, holding him to her even as part of her wanted him to just take her and ease this fierce ache.

Finally he lifted his head and cupped both breasts in his hands, massaging them. She moaned and spread her legs, practically begging for him there.

He kissed down her belly, making her quiver, and then to her hip and down her leg, surprising her. No man had ever kissed her legs. It had always been boobs and pleasure town. He pushed her leg open and kissed behind her knee, making her jolt at the unexpectedly sensitive spot. His mouth was magic—perfect firmness, perfect pressure, like the most perfect kisses but on the rest of her. She moaned and ached and reveled in the pleasure he gave so generously.

He worked his way back up to her inner thigh, his fingers finally touching where she needed him most in one long sure stroke and then inside. He lifted his finger. "You're so wet." He sucked that finger in an erotic gesture that made her grab his shoulders, desperately trying to pull him up her body and inside her. She couldn't budge him.

"Now, now," she urged.

"Shh," he murmured, pushing her other leg to the side and kissing along the inside of her thigh while his fingers stroked her intimately, learning her by feel again, *everywhere.* She trembled with need.

His fingers left her aching sex and shifted to stroke up her side as he maneuvered himself back up her body, kissing and tasting along the way. Her hips moved restlessly, not used to so much waiting. And it had been so-o-o long. Finally he was fully in position, between her legs, his head hovering just over hers.

His thumb stroked her lower lip. "You're so beautiful, so sexy."

Her heart squeezed at his generosity, taking such care with her. She stroked his jaw, just a hint of scruff on it. "You too," she managed.

He kissed her, another long and deep kiss that would've swept her off her feet had she been standing. Finally he broke the kiss and eased his body off her, getting out of bed.

"Wait!" She reached for him.

He took her hand and kissed the palm. "Getting protection."

She closed her eyes, her cheeks flushing with embarrass- ment over her desperate need to have him. And then he was back, his heat and weight so welcome.

He kissed her and spoke against her lips. "Wrap your legs up high around my waist. It'll make it easier for you. Open you up."

"Oh, God." She did as he said.

He didn't thrust, more like eased himself in, giving her

body time to adjust. He kissed her forehead, then her nose, then her mouth. "I love how tight you are," he said against her lips.

She sighed and then he slid home, stealing her breath.

He cradled her face with one hand, still and restrained. "You doing okay?"

She nodded happily and grabbed his ass. "You don't have to hold back anymore."

He grazed his lips over hers. "This won't be quick. We've both waited for this."

Their gazes locked. Her breath came faster, every part of her alive and aware, filled like she'd never felt before. She tightened her inner muscles around him and they both groaned. He started moving then, deep thrusts that made her ache, nearly leaving her before filling her again. It made her wild. She urged him on, but he kissed her, his tongue thrusting in her mouth, quieting her. She felt taken, claimed by his mouth and powerful thrusts, carried along by his sure strokes. The orgasm snuck up on her, making her gasp into his mouth and he kept going, faster now, his head lifting to watch her as he took her in hard thrusts that brought wave after wave of pleasure. His head snapped back, the cords of his neck strained, and then he let go with a harsh primal sound that sent another pulse of pleasure through her.

He stilled, giving her his weight for a long moment before lifting his head and kissing her soundly on the mouth.

"Mmm," she said and closed her eyes in satiated bliss.

He shifted to the mattress next to her. Then he reached over and held her hand.

A slow smile spread across her face so big she could feel it at the corners of her eyes. She floated in a rare state of absolute contentment. Perfection.

∼

Ethan was *not* a desperate man, particularly where women were concerned. He was the king of cool, troubles rolled off his shoulders, and he moved right along.

But the minute Ally rolled out of his bed, where he'd just had the best sex of his life, with a cheery "thank you!" he veered embarrassingly close to desperate. The hair on the back of his neck stood on end, his fingers tingled with the need to touch, to hold her close even after sexual satisfaction, and his dormant heart lurched to life with a pang of longing so intense he had to force himself not to grab her and haul her back to bed.

"Don't thank me," he growled, propping up on one elbow.

She looked around, still gloriously naked, probably trying to locate her bra, which he'd heaved a distance away. "Can you get up? I need you to drive me home." She pulled on her panties and jeans, then looked under the bed and straightened suddenly, making her gorgeous breasts bounce. "Where's my bra?"

He faked a yawn and lay flat on his back. "I'm tired. Can I take you home in the morning?"

She leaned over him, her luscious breasts brushing his chest, tempting him. "I'm so sorry, but it's a school night. Stay awake, okay?" Her soft hair trailed over his cheek and he pushed it back behind her ear before cradling her head. "I have work in the morning, and spending the night feels like more than…"

His voice came out hoarse. "More than what?"

She straightened, pushing off the bed. "Never mind. I'll call Missy or Lexi for a ride. Sabrina will ask too many questions."

He wrapped his fingers around her wrist before she could make her escape, stroking the underside with his thumb. She stared at his hand.

He worked on enticing her. "If I make it worth your while, will you stay?" *Said the lion to the lamb.*

"What would make it worth my while?" Her voice was all breathy. Awesome.

He smirked. "What all women want."

"You know what all women want?"

He gave a tug, pulling her on top of him.

"Eth!" She propped up on his chest and gave him a disgruntled look.

He framed her face with his hands. "Stay till morning and I'll show you. I promise to get you to work on time."

Her eyes went soft and she quickly looked away, focusing on a spot near his ear. "This isn't a relationship if I spend the night."

He stroked her back, soothing her. She was skittish; he understood why now. He wanted to throttle Dean but, at the same time, thank him for letting Ally go. She didn't belong with a man who couldn't deal with the consequences of his actions.

She belonged with him.

He cupped the back of her neck, drew her down, and kissed her gently. "We don't need a label."

She relaxed, shifting to his side. "Okay, I'll spend the night." She shimmied off her jeans and tossed them.

He let out a quiet breath of relief, turned off the light on the nightstand, made sure the blanket was on both of them, and pulled her close, wrapping an arm around her shoulders. She cuddled up against his side, resting her head on his chest right over his heart.

With no prompting from him, she got chatty, telling him all about her new goals, dreams, and quest for fulfilling experiences now that she was solo married. He liked that she confided in him. He didn't even raise a peep of concern when she said she was seriously thinking of taking that job with Claire. She was ready for adventure. He let her get it all out, making sure he responded with encouraging comments when appropriate, but all he could think was, get it out of your system. Go nuts. And then come back to me.

Because this wasn't a onetime thing.

All cuddled up like that, her softness pressed close, filled him with satisfaction. He'd intended another round or two, but the sheer contentment of holding her made him relax into a deep sleep.

He woke early as usual and took her in, her blond hair mussed, her cheeks pink, her lashes resting on her soft cheeks, her sexy mouth with the dip at the top lip and the fullness of her lower lip, those luscious breasts.

Her eyes fluttered open. "Hi."

He smiled, his chest aching like his heart would burst at this moment he'd longed for with every cell in his being—waking up with a woman who made him smile. "Hi."

"What time is it?"

"Still early. Only six."

She stretched. "I usually get up at seven."

"Gives us time for what women want."

"And just how do you know this fact?" she asked, all saucy.

He kissed her smiling mouth. "Spread your legs for me, beautiful."

Her breath hitched and she immediately threw back the covers, pulled off her panties, and did as he asked. He went rock hard and then had to rein himself in with the tight restraint needed to control himself. He'd always been barely leashed energy. Ally was special and deserved what tenderness he could give.

He started with gentle kisses on her sexy mouth, pausing frequently to gaze into her wide blue eyes, so open and trusting despite her best efforts to protect herself. She didn't have it in her to turn off her open loving nature. He reminded himself to take care. When he was sure he had enough control, he shifted down her body, proving he knew exactly what he was talking about. Yeah, he went down on her. All women wanted that. Just like all guys loved a blowjob.

And she loved it. Her nails dug into his shoulders, her hips rose up to meet him, she moaned and whimpered, and he held her to his pace, slowing down when she was close, more aggressive when she relaxed. When he finally pushed her over the edge, she bowed off the mattress with a keening cry.

When he rose up over her and grinned, she grabbed him and hugged him tight, thanking him profusely. That only made him want to do it more. But she begged him to fuck her, so what could he do?

Much later, she cheerfully made them both breakfast, French toast with scrambled eggs, all while telling him about her first-grade class and the plans she had for the week. He made the coffee, practically whistling to himself. It was clear she loved kids despite her restless quest for life outside the classroom. Like him, she had a lot of energy. He could easily picture her raising wild energetic kids who hiked and fished and camped. His blood, his family.

Rein it in.

She joined him at the table a short while later and, even though he usually just had coffee in the morning, he ate everything with gusto. She asked him about himself and he gave her small pieces of it, his closeness with the Campbell family and his foster brother, Zach, his satisfaction with his job, his tight ties to the community. She already understood about his love for the outdoors. He left out the harsher side of his life—his crummy childhood bouncing from the orphanage to a series of foster homes. Left out the seedier side of his job —the arrests that had turned violent, requiring him to subdue the perp, the ugly domestic situations he'd been called into. He wouldn't sully her. He wanted to keep her just like this— untouched by the harsher side of life. Besides, no one wanted to hear the sob story of an orphan who'd never been adopted. It made him look pathetic, the boy nobody wanted. He'd made a man of himself through sheer determination and the support of his chosen family, the Campbells.

"You ever been camping?" he asked.

"I did an overnight with the Girl Scouts once," she replied. "We all slept in a huge log cabin like a giant slumber party."

"No, I mean real camping. Like sleeping under the stars."

"On the ground?" she asked, crinkling her nose. "Like all exposed to bears and bugs and snakes?" She shuddered.

"Could be in a tent." He offered a more civilized version, though he preferred real camping—ground underneath, sky above.

"Sounds rough."

"It's fun. Great to get away from civilization and back to the basics."

She grinned. "As long as the basics include a bathroom with a shower, I'm game."

"City slicker," he teased.

"I'll have you know I'm a suburb girl through and through."

"Could be an adventure," he said, playing to her quest for new experiences. "Call of the wild. Bring out all your primitive instincts." He smirked, thinking how awesome sex in the great outdoors with Ally would be.

"I can be primitive just as easily in a soft bed if you're with me." She gave him a sweet smile. "You made me feel so good. Thank you."

He flushed with pride, his chest bursting with happiness. He leaned across the table, hooked his fingers around the back of her neck and pulled her in for a kiss. "My pleasure." He released her and settled back into his chair. "Still think a vibrator is better than a man?"

She beamed radiantly, pure sunshine. "It's like you said before when we both agreed men suck—you're the exception."

Pure satisfaction washed through him. "Thanks." He soaked her in, hoping he could keep this thing going long enough to actually reel her in because he was already sunk.

12

———

Ally stopped by the supermarket after work, finally calming down from what she was now calling the night (and morning after) that Ethan blew her mind. Only took eleven hours for her to calm down. Ha! The man was a collection of contradictions—tough with a stone expression that rarely cracked into a smile, but then in bed he'd been gentle, almost tender. She'd never experienced that with any man. And the way he'd listened, really listened, to her relationship concerns. He was the most amazing man she'd ever met.

No pulling the rug out from under you, I promise. I like you and want to spend time with you. Ethan's words came back to her again, bringing a gooey deep affection. She was halfway in love with him.

Oh, God. She was falling for him.

She gave herself a mental shake, pushing her cart down the bread aisle. *Focus.* She'd spoken to Claire about the assistant opportunity after work today only to find it wasn't a good fit. So what was she going to do with her life? What was her purpose? This thinking-things-through stuff wasn't for the faint of heart.

Her cart was full of healthy food when she made her final stop at the freezer section for ice cream. She halted two steps down the aisle. As if conjured from her thoughts, Ethan stood at the opposite end of the aisle.

She made herself continue forward like everything was normal. Like her heart wasn't racing, her knees wobbly over seeing him so soon after their hookup. Nothing like the early evening after the morning after…whatever. It was always awkward to see your lover fully dressed when the vision of their naked body was still fresh in mind. The things his mouth had done to her. She throbbed at the memory.

He hadn't noticed her yet as he picked out Hungry Guy frozen dinners.

Just be friendly. Casual. No big deal.

"There's my stalker!" she called with a wave.

He straightened and flashed a smile that stopped her heart. She flushed and her heart kicked into high gear as she closed the distance between them, parking her cart alongside his.

He tossed two more frozen dinners into his cart, joining the pile already in there. "Yeah, I figured if I stood here long enough, you were bound to come in for…"

"Ice cream," she supplied. "And ya know, the usual stuff for the week."

He searched her features for a moment before asking, "How's the plan to work with Claire? Have you spoken to her about it?"

She sighed. "It's not going to work out. She says after the movie wraps, she and Jake want to buy a horse farm in Connecticut. They're hoping to start a family. She said she'll still be working, but probably more behind the camera with her production company."

"So she doesn't need an assistant?"

"No, she does, but it would be more local." She frowned. "I don't want to hang around a horse farm in Connecticut. I've lived my whole life in Connecticut. I thought it would be so glam too. I told her that and she understood. She said she'd ask around if another actress needs an assistant that would involve more travel for me. She knows, like, everyone."

Ethan moved to stand by her side. "Sorry it didn't work out, but I'm glad you'll be sticking around."

"Thanks. But there's still a possibility. Claire could come through with something else. She has incredible connections."

His voice turned husky, making her knees weak. "You free for dinner on Saturday night?"

"Yes."

He smiled warmly. "Then it's a date."

Her self-preservation kicked in, needing to slow it down, protect her heart. "But I'm not spending the night this time."

He arched a brow. "Not even for what women want?"

She hesitated, but told herself to remain firm with the boundaries. "Not even that."

"All right." He played with a lock of her hair. "I've got another thing you might like."

That got her attention. No, she needed firm boundaries. Besides, next Sunday morning was Lauren's bachelorette brunch. Her friend was such a sweetheart, she wanted her bachelorette party to be a classy brunch at a nice restaurant. There'd been much debate among her friends over secretly springing a stripper on Lauren at the brunch, but Hailey had put a quick halt to those proceedings, declaring they'd be kicked out of the restaurant for that. They'd settled for the much tamer mimosas with secret gifts of naughty lingerie. Ally personally thought that was more a gift for Lauren's fiancé than Lauren, but it would be fun to watch her blush and attempt to thank everyone in her usual sweet way.

"I have plans Sunday morning," she informed him, but then she couldn't resist. "Tell me the other thing I might like."

He pushed her hair behind her ear. "You'll have to spend the night to find out. I'll make sure you're not late for your plans."

She narrowed her eyes. This sounded like a trick. He just wanted to cuddle her and that was bound to get her all mushy and vulnerable.

"Up to you," he said with a smirk. "Last woman I did it too actually…nah. You don't need to know that."

She slammed a hand on her hip. "Not cool to talk about

other women with the woman you're currently proposition-ing, you know."

He shrugged and watched her with a confident sexy look in his eyes.

Ooh, she couldn't take the suspense. "What'd she do?"

He leaned down and whispered near her ear, the words hot against her skin. "She turtled."

"She what?"

He stroked her hair back from her ear and held it as he cradled the side of her head and whispered, "She made this wheezy sound like a turtle orgasm."

She was so confused. Also intrigued. And a hot mess of hormones. "And you know about turtle orgasms how?"

He dropped his hand and met her eyes. "YouTube video. Guys at work showed me."

"So you didn't actually witness turtles fucking while you were doing your park ranger thing?"

He grinned and looked around. Luckily, they were alone down at this end of the aisle, because she'd said that turtles-fucking thing a little loud. "That would be a no," he said. "And I'm not a park ranger."

She crossed her arms. "I'm not sure I want to turtle."

He gave her his sexiest smirk. "Bark? Meow? Howl?"

She laughed and uncrossed her arms.

He took her hand in a firm clasp. "I'll pick you up at six on Saturday. Dinner will be all suburban-like with running water and a chef that prepares the meal."

She melted. "Okay. Will there be benefits after?"

"Up to you," he said at the same time as he nodded.

She laughed. "All right, it's a..." She coughed, nearly choking on the word. She was so afraid she was going to get her hopes up again, go all Cinderella on his ass when there simply was no prince waiting to whisk her away to ever-lasting happiness. Real life didn't work that way.

"Date," he supplied.

She took a shaky breath. And then put as much cheer into her voice as she could while she babbled nervously. "Yes. Well, I better get going. I have a lot of cooking to do. I'm making white chicken chili for dinner and three loaves of pumpkin bread for my class tomorrow."

He didn't move, still close enough to make her want to throw herself at him. "It's a nice place; dress would be good."

She nodded in a jerky motion, waved him to the side and, as soon as he moved, she grabbed her cart and made a U-turn out of the frozen aisle, her stomach doing a jittery dance.

It wasn't until she got home that she realized she forgot the ice cream.

Ethan rarely did the fancy-dinner thing. Not his style. But he needed Ally to know he was serious about her. Casual hookups didn't get across that message. Not that he'd turn down hooking up with her. He just...dammit, if he was going to do this, he had to do it right. Full-on wooing. He'd never wooed in his life, but his foster brother, Zach, was a professor of anthropology and had shared some good stuff about dating based on real anthropological evidence and biology. He'd explained the dominant male was highly valued for a mate as protector and provider for the young. Dominant didn't mean pressing the other person down. It was more like strength to fight off enemies and rivals, protect the family and bring home the gift of food. Though Ally brought her own food home and cooked better than he did. Whatever. It had made sense at the time. He was a cop, so he already had the protector thing down.

He peered in the bathroom mirror at the crappy knot in his tie and undid it again. If she understood him at all, she'd know what a big deal this fancy dinner was. He tied the knot again and then loosened it. He hated ties.

He finished getting ready, nerves making him tense and jumpy. He couldn't remember being nervous about a date since he was a teenager on his first date. It felt like so much was riding on it. He was serious about Ally, had tried to be as straightforward as possible about that, but it still felt like any moment she was going to slip through his fingers. Like he'd turn around and she be flying off to Paris for a year as some movie star's assistant or off to Japan to teach kids English or something.

But he couldn't back off. Not when he felt so much. He thought about her a lot—her cheerful exuberance, her beaming smile, her grit, her luscious body, her softness. When he wasn't with her, he couldn't wait to see her again. And when he saw her, the whole world was brighter, sights and sounds sharper. He closed his eyes and took a deep breath in and out. What the hell happened to him? He'd only known her up close and personal for four weeks. That was much too soon for…love. Had it finally happened for him? He'd never felt like this before, all out of sorts and wanting another person close so much. He suspected it was, but wouldn't check in with anyone to ask. He'd just move forward like everything was normal.

Because if Ally didn't love him back, there was no point in even thinking about it.

He loved her.

Fuck.

He'd never told anyone he loved them. And no one had ever said it to him. Would that bad luck streak finally end?

Or would he be waving goodbye as she left for some grand adventure?

He shrugged on the suit blazer. Enough thinking. Time for action. He marched out the door.

Ally was standing in a bra and panties, carefully applying mascara in the bathroom mirror, when the doorbell rang. Shit. He was early! She yanked the bands out of her two braids, tousled her hair into the kinky waves she'd been going for and then raced to her bedroom for her pink fleece robe. "Coming!" Now that she lived alone, she couldn't count on her roomie to run interference.

She rushed to the door, peeked through the peephole, and yanked it open, a little breathless. "Hey, you're way early."

Ethan stepped inside, looking somber and serious in a navy blue suit. "I was ready. I don't mind waiting for you. Take your time." His gaze dropped to her bare legs, where the robe ended mid-thigh, and then traveled up to the gaping top that likely gave him an eyeful of cleavage. Finally, he lifted lust-filled eyes to hers.

Her body responded in kind with a throbbing pulse between her legs. She licked her lips, closed the distance between them and placed a hand on his chest. "Nice tie."

"Ally," he said in a strained voice.

"Eth," she whispered.

They slammed together, mouths hungry, hands grabbing. She was frantic for him, pushing off his blazer, grabbing his shirt and lifting it from his pants, undoing his belt buckle, all while his mouth devoured hers. He kept kissing her, shifting her to the wall, pressing and grinding against her. She was wild to have him, lifting her leg and wrapping it around his, tilting her hips up in invitation. He slid a hand under her robe and cupped her between the legs, where she was already hot and wet. He kissed her harder, more demanding, and then tore his mouth away, his fingers hooked on the sides of her panties.

"Stop me," he said.

She pushed his hands off and slid the panties down herself. Then she opened her robe and tossed it to the side.

He groaned.

The rest happened shockingly fast. He freed himself, lifted her and took her in one fierce thrust, her back hitting cool wall. She gasped at the sudden filling of her body and then there was nothing but his mouth on hers, his body pumping hard and fierce, the intense coiling of tension at her core, higher and higher. She broke the kiss, desperate for breath, and he held her by the cheek and jaw, his eyes hot on hers, his thrusts deep and incredibly powerful, like he held nothing back this time. He gave her everything, the hard and the tender, and she understood in that moment who he was. Tough on the outside, tender on the inside. But she couldn't speak, could only hang on, panting and aching and completely overwhelmed. His hand slipped between them, stroking her rapidly, and she jerked and then exploded, the orgasm stealing her breath. He pounded into her and she just clung to him. His own release pulsed inside her moments later, bringing another wave of pleasure.

He leaned his forehead against hers, breathing heavily. "You okay?"

"Yeah."

He lifted his head and smiled tenderly. Her heart squeezed painfully hard. He kissed her gently. "Sorry if I was rough."

"I like it both ways, rough and gentle. It's like you, tough on the outside, secretly tender on the inside. Right?"

"I dunno. Maybe." He lifted her off him, set her down, and retrieved her robe, wrapping it around her shoulders.

That was when she felt the aftermath—no-doubt virile sperm sliding out of her. Her stomach dropped and she went cold all over. How could she have let this happen again? How could he after he knew about her accidental pregnancy?

He tucked himself back into his pants and zipped up.

She slid her arms into the sleeves of the robe and tied it with shaking fingers.

"What's wrong?"

Her voice came out small. "You didn't use a condom."

His face fell. "Ally, oh, God, I'm so sorry." He pulled her close, hugging her. She couldn't hug him back. She was stiff and cold. He rubbed her back. "I wasn't thinking. I'm clean. I always use protection."

"It's okay," she said through numb lips. Though nothing was okay.

He pulled back to look at her. "You're shaking. C'mere. Sit down." He tried to guide her to the sofa, but she pulled away.

"I'm fine."

"Ally, I'm really sorry." His voice was a quiet misery. "I just wanted tonight to be perfect, and I screwed up."

"It's not your fault. We were both stupid." She headed toward her bedroom. "Give me a few minutes to get ready."

"Ally…"

She stopped, numbly waiting for him to finish his sentence.

"I'm not like Dean. I'll deal with the consequences of my actions."

She nodded stiffly and retreated to her room. His reassurance just made her feel worse. Like it was a bad thing if she got pregnant. Of course it was. They weren't in a committed relationship.

She sat on her bed, the numb shock wearing off. She didn't take risks like that. Ever. Not since Dean.

She closed her eyes and took a few deep breaths. She was expecting her period in a couple of days. Chances of a pregnancy were smaller; ovulation had most likely passed. Well, she'd know in a couple of days, wouldn't she?

Ethan appeared in her doorway, his face creased with worry. "Do you want to skip dinner?"

She shook her head. "No, let's go. I'm expecting my period in two days. I'm sure it'll be fine."

He visibly relaxed. "Okay. I'll go wait in the living room."

She quickly dressed, not giving herself time to dwell on the uncertainty. She'd enjoy a nice meal with good company, even if they were complete morons when they got too close. Not like they were going to hook up again after that scare. Talk about a buzzkill.

She stepped out to the living room in her little black dress and black heels. "Ready," she said, putting as much cheer into her voice as she could.

"Hope you like French food," he said, heading to the front door and opening it for her.

"Mmm, French fries are my favorite."

He barked out a laugh. "Not sure they're on the menu."

They headed down the outdoor hallway toward the stairs. "How about French toast?"

"Actually, that is on the menu."

"Ha!"

"They've got all the usual culprits. You'll be well fed." He entwined his fingers with hers and they were off for a date she was determined to enjoy.

13

———

French food to the rescue. Ethan breathed a sigh of relief because Ally was enjoying herself so much. The place was intimate with lots of tables for two covered in white table-cloths with a glowing candle and too much silverware. Ally exclaimed over every course, which was a lot. They both got the prix fixe menu with a bunch of tiny courses. Ally got hers with a glass of wine, her cheeks glowing, from wine or sex he wasn't sure, but he soaked her in greedily. His life had never seen so much sweetness and light as it had since she came into it. He'd been so worried he'd screwed up earlier, fucking her rough before their date and not even using protection. He knew better, especially after she'd confided in him about her lost pregnancy. He had to be more careful with her physically and emotionally. He was embarrassingly inexperienced at this love stuff. But, dammit, he would die trying.

They shared a chocolate soufflé, which Ally looked so orgasmic over, he purposely slowed down eating to let her have more of it. She sped up correspondingly and finished it off with a blissful sigh that made his chest fill with warmth. Her happiness was everything.

She wiped her mouth carefully with a napkin. "I'm glad we went to dinner. This was wonderful. Thank you."

"You're welcome." He considered his next steps. He

wanted to spend the night with her, even if it didn't involve sex, and he didn't want another desperate negotiation to convince her. "What're your plans for tomorrow morning?"

"Lauren's bachelorette brunch. Actually, it's not far from here." They were in the wealthy town of Greenport. "So no strippers, as you can imagine." She made a small pout.

"I could show up as a cop stripper," he offered with a straight face.

Her eyes widened. "That would be awesome!"

He shook his head, laughing. "I was kidding."

"I'd bet you'd earn a lot of money as a side gig doing that," she said enthusiastically.

"Thanks?"

She laughed.

He leaned across the table and lowered his voice. "Tell me why you're against spending the night."

Her smile dropped and she fiddled with her napkin. "I'm not against it per se. I just don't want to make it a habit."

He straightened, figuring he could work with that. "Once a week isn't much of a habit. What time's your brunch?"

She leaned across the table and whispered, "Why do you want to spend the night together? I can't imagine you're in the mood after our screwup."

He leaned close and whispered back, "I'm always in the mood, but that's not why. I like waking up to someone who makes me smile."

Her lips curved into a small smile, her eyes soft. "Eth." She swallowed visibly. "That was so sweet." She kissed him and straightened. "Okay, you can stay at my place. Brunch is at eleven, so I'll probably be up around nine."

He relaxed, glad he'd said the right thing. It was the truth too. "Works for me."

"Did you guys do anything fun for Alex's bachelor party? Lauren told us you all went into the city last night."

"No strippers there either."

"Bummer, right?"

He shook his head, smiling. She was probably the only

woman in the world who'd feel sorry for them not having strippers. "Doesn't do much for me anyway."

"Su-ure," she said with a big exaggerated nod. "You're the exception."

He flashed a smile. "That's right. We went to Chelsea Piers and did the batting cages, driving range, and rock-climbing wall. Then we headed over to Marcus's bar to hang out in the private room. Played some pool and poker."

"Lame-o."

He snorted. "It was fun, really, but definitely not your typical bachelor party. *And* he called her twice because he missed her. So whipped."

She cocked her head. "I don't know, I think that's kind of sweet. Did you get him a present?"

"We all chipped in for Chelsea Piers and his drinks. Was I supposed to get him something else too?"

"I don't know how bachelor parties work, but definitely for a bachelorette party. We're all getting her naughty lingerie."

He leaned in, intrigued. "Naughty, huh? What's your contribution? Better yet, what naughty lingerie do you wear?"

She gave him an impish smile that told him she definitely wore some good stuff. "I got her a black lace bustier that exposes her midriff, with teeny string bikini panties. You know what a bustier is?"

"It's a fancy boob holder."

"Yeah, it's like—" she cupped near her breasts and he quickly glanced around to make sure no pervs were watching besides him "—from here down your sides. It sort of lifts your boobs like an enticing offering."

Her dirty talk was turning him on. He loved that she was so open. "Do you have one of those?"

She leaned across the table and he leaned in too. "I hope this isn't TMI but, after a breakup, I throw out any lingerie I wore with my ex. I told you it's been a while for me. I haven't bought any in years. No guy really interested me."

He smiled big time. "Until me."

She pursed her lips. "Don't let it go to your head."

He grinned and leaned back in his seat. "You know, I'm glad you tossed the old stuff. I don't want some other guy's imprint where I want mine."

"Imprint," she said and laughed.

He smiled. "I'm trying to be classy." He looked around at all the couples dressed formally and speaking in low tones. "This is a classy place." And she went right there with him with the dirty talk.

The waiter arrived, offered coffee, which they both turned down, and left the check. Once that was taken care of, he helped Ally from her chair and walked her out, the lingerie conversation still stuck in his mind. What kind of lingerie would Ally wear?

As soon as they were safely in the privacy of his car, still parked on the street, he turned to her. "Would you wear lingerie for me?"

She smiled brightly. "Sure, what kind do you like? Bustier, teddy, slip, romper, or bodysuit?"

"Yes."

"That's not very specific. Ooh, I know! Come on, there's a lingerie shop in town. Just a few blocks away." She hopped out of the Jeep.

Aw, man. He hated shopping. He'd hoped she'd just show up one night in something skimpy. He met up with her on the sidewalk and she grabbed his hand, practically running toward the shop. "We have to hurry," she said. "They might be closing soon."

They got there and the sign on the front door said they closed at nine. "Yes!" Ally cheered. "We've got twenty minutes. When you see something you like, just holler."

It didn't even have a dirty name like Barely There Nudes or Hot and Skimpy like he'd hoped. It was called Deborah Marshall. Right there his hopes took a dive.

He followed Ally inside to an explosion of pink and white. Pink walls, white carpet, pink shelves and pink hangers. Headless mannequins modeled the latest lacy things. It smelled like flowers. If any of the guys saw him in here, they'd never let him live it down.

They were the only customers. A bored thin woman in her fifties with black cat's-eye glasses hanging on a chain around her neck and a prim buttoned-up white shirt stood behind the register. Maybe that was who the shop was named after. "May I help you?" she called.

"Just looking, thanks," Ally replied.

He leaned down to Ally's ear. "Get whatever you want. I'll wait outside."

She grabbed his hand and dragged him along. "I need to know what you like. I'm only wearing it for you."

His heart kerthunked. "I like black. The skimpier the better."

He'd thought that would narrow it down, but it turned out the world of women's lingerie was much more complicated than he'd realized. Honestly, it all looked good to him. He watched Ally's expression as she quickly went through all the black items, and when she got excited over what she called a slip and he called a thin dress, he told her that was his favorite. She was so excited she did a little dance, holding it up for him to feel how soft the satin was. He was more interested in the sheer lace over the breasts along with the deep plunge both in front and back.

They took it to the counter and he pulled out his credit card. "My gift," he told her.

"Thank you," Ally said. "I'll get you the guy version."

He smiled. "This is the guy version. A gift for you is a gift for me. Trust me on that."

She squeezed him around the middle in a hug. He put an arm around her shoulders and gave her a little squeeze back.

The salesclerk slid her glasses on and peered at them. "What an adorable couple." She turned to him. "Would you like the matching sheer robe?"

This place was pricey. He considered the high dollar value of the combined outfit that Ally would throw away if they broke up and then decided in an optimistic burst that he didn't have to worry about that.

Ally shook her head. "That's okay."

"We'll take it," he said.

Ally squeaked and hugged him around the middle again. Worth it.

Ally had enjoyed their night out, but now that they were back at her place, she was hiding in the bathroom, heart racing, hands trembling in the black satin and lace slip and sheer robe. Ethan was lounging in her bed, probably naked, waiting to see her model the lingerie.

Why did she let him spend the night? She was only getting herself in deeper. She needed space not more togetherness. She could practically feel the inevitable crash about to slam into her when this all went south. Yet when she imagined coming home to an empty apartment after their tumultuous night, she knew exactly why she allowed him to stay. She wasn't ready to let him go. As simple as that.

Ethan was grounded and solid in a way her ex-boyfriends had never been. She didn't know if it was because he was a cop or because he was a little older than her ex-boyfriends. In any case, she liked his solidness, liked that he was someone she could count on. When he made a promise, she believed him. She wasn't nearly as freaked as she should've been at the possibility of an accidental pregnancy. Because it was Ethan. He was husband material. *Dammit!* She hated that her mind went there, even with her new enlightened attitude about making her own happiness.

She loved him.

Her stomach did a topsy-turvy flip. She loved the tough guy and didn't have a clue if he felt the same way. He cared for her, liked her, definitely, but love? She told herself not to put any heavy expectations out there. The future would take care of itself one way or the other.

Maybe she'd be pregnant, maybe she wouldn't.

Maybe he'd bail, maybe he'd stay a while longer and then bail.

Maybe she'd stay in this bathroom forever.

She gave herself a last look in the mirror, her worry written all over her face. She turned away, leaving the bathroom and making her slow way into the bedroom on shaky legs.

He'd left the light on the nightstand on, probably to see her outfit. He was definitely naked, sitting up in her bed, the pillow bunched behind him. He looked out of place—all hard sculpted muscle—in her girly bed with its coral paisleys and flowers comforter. Normally she went to her boyfriend's place because she used to always have a roommate.

He wolf-whistled. "Beautiful. So beautiful."

She stopped next to the bed and blurted, "I'm scared."

He threw the cover back and pulled her in, wrapping his arms around her so they were lying side by side, facing each other, and then stroked her hair back from her face. "Don't be scared. What're you scared of?"

"Everything. You, me, the future."

"It'll be okay." He kissed her forehead, her cheek, the spot just below her ear that made her melt. "Don't worry, okay?" he said in a husky coaxing voice by her ear. "Just enjoy." He nuzzled her neck, bringing a hot shiver.

She let out a shuddering breath. "I'll try."

He rolled on top of her in one smooth move, settling between her legs, his mouth claiming hers, his hard warm weight at once comforting and arousing. His tongue took possession, his fingers tangled in her hair, carrying her away to the realm of pleasure, and she let him.

14

The bride looked like a princess, the groom her handsome prince, and the flower girl—Lauren's two-year-old stepdaughter, Viv—was so freaking adorable Ally's uterus hurt. Ally waited in the back of St. Joseph's Church with the bridal party to walk down the aisle for Lauren and Alex's big day, the catch in her throat over the emotional occasion purely for the happy bride, not because she wished she was also a bride. Okay, old habits died hard. This beautiful occasion was exactly how Ally had pictured her own wedding, but the groom's face had always been blurry in those fantasies. That should've given her a clue that her ex-boyfriends were not the One, but now she wasn't waiting for the One. She was the One.

She sighed. She hadn't seen or heard from Ethan since last Sunday morning when she'd headed out to Lauren's bachelorette brunch. Six days ago. He wasn't one of those guys who called or texted just because he missed her. Maybe he didn't miss her at all. He got in touch only to schedule a time to meet up. When she saw him, he was great, tender and caring, but then when they were apart, which was most of the time, it was like he forgot about her. Absence might make the heart grow fonder, but it made her feel hurt and put aside. Like she was only a sometimes thing when it was convenient. She hated that her emotions were all tangled up. She'd been trying to do things differently this time, better.

At the very least he could've checked in to see if she was pregnant. Not pregnant, thanks so much for your concern.

Organ music began inside the church. Hailey, both maid-of-honor and the wedding planner, walked over and took Viv's hand. The little girl had been bouncing all around the bride, wearing her special Princess Kei-Kei dress, a character from a beloved animated movie—pink satin with a pink tutu covered in a pattern of neon green elves. The neon green continued on large bows on her shoulders and waist. And, like any self-respecting princess, she wore a rhinestone tiara. She clutched the handle of a small basket of red rose petals in one hand. The princess fantasy started young.

Hailey leaned down to Viv. "It's time. You remember what to do? Walk slowly to your daddy and *gently* toss the petals."

Viv nodded vigorously, her tiara bouncing askew on her wavy light brown hair. Hailey fixed the tiara before opening the church door for her and gesturing for her to go.

Viv hurried through the open door and into the aisle.

They all gathered close, watching through the door that Hailey propped open with a small doorstop.

Viv was doing beautifully, walking instead of running like she had at rehearsal last night, and tossing fistfuls of rose petals to her left at regular intervals. Everyone *awwed* and whispered because she was just so dang cute.

Unfortunately, she ran out of petals halfway down the aisle and came to a dead stop, turning the basket upside down and shaking it.

Alex Campbell, the groom and Viv's daddy, gestured for her to blow kisses instead.

Viv shook her head, turned and stomped back toward the bridal party still waiting their turn to go down the aisle, with a disgruntled expression on her face.

The crowd tittered, craning their necks to see what she'd do next.

Alex rubbed the back of his neck. The groomsmen were all grinning. Ethan wasn't among them or she would've given him a good glare. Alex had had to limit the number of brothers in his lineup.

Viv headed straight to Lauren, showing her the upside-down basket. "All gone!"

Sweet Lauren pulled a red rose from her own bouquet, handing it to Viv. "This is a super special flower so you need to hold it carefully. Don't throw this one, okay?"

Viv stared at the rose in awe and tossed the basket behind her.

Ally set the basket out of the way and pulled a white carnation from her own bouquet. "Here you go."

Everyone quickly followed suit. Viv's eyes were wide as she clutched her very own bouquet of white and red flowers in both hands. Hailey appeared in a rush from a side door, holding a white satin ribbon that she used to quickly tie the flower stems together.

"Go, flower girl," Hailey said, lifting Viv and depositing her at the end of the aisle again.

Viv walked jauntily down the aisle, holding her bouquet in front of her and beaming.

A chorus of *aww*s struck again.

Viv *almost* made it down the aisle.

Ally cringed. At this rate Lauren was never going to get her turn down the aisle. Just before Viv made it to the groom, she veered right, dropped the bouquet, and climbed into her grandfather's lap.

"Close enough," Lauren announced. "Let's roll."

Ally stood in the ballroom of Ludbury House, a sprawling two-and-a-half-story white clapboard mansion with white columns and a beautiful wraparound porch just across the street from the church, for the reception. Like all of historic Ludbury House, the ballroom was spectacular, lit with an elaborate gold and crystal chandelier in the center of the room over a hardwood dance floor. Round tables with white table-cloths and colorful floral centerpieces surrounded the dance floor, and tall white candles glowed on long tables on the far side of the room, where appetizers and drinks waited. Ally had seen Ethan filing in with the guys and had gotten a smile and a raised hand of acknowledgment from across the room, but nothing more.

Hailey sailed by. "We're getting ready for the bride and groom's special dance. Then everyone from the bridal party."

Ally was paired up across the aisle with Ben Wright. He caught her eye and winked at her. She gave him a thumbs-up. That one had trouble written all over him. He was a flirt with a mischievous twinkly look in his eyes and a dimpled smile he used liberally. She imagined he left a string of broken hearts wherever he went.

The music started and the DJ announced the first dance of the bride and groom. Lauren and Alex moved perfectly together. Lauren was tall and graceful, Alex a smooth and confident lead. The bridal party was big, though it could've been huge if Hailey hadn't stepped in as wedding planner and explained the logistical difficulty of getting all of Lauren's friends and Alex's brothers up at the altar. They ended up with Hailey and Lauren's sister, Anne, both as maid of honor, and Carrie, Ally, Mad, and Claire as bridesmaids. Of course, with movie star Claire in attendance, the curtains had to be closed in the ballroom and a full security detail on guard both inside and out to keep away paparazzi. In any case, the large bridal party was mostly to match up with Alex's groomsmen, his biological brothers, best man Josh, then Jake, Ty, Logan, and the two honorary brothers closest to his age, Park and Ben. The couples were partnered up across the aisle —Claire and Jake, Mad and Park—the rest of them paired randomly. Josh and Hailey did not pair up. That was definitely not random.

Her gaze drifted, seeking out Ethan again in his dark gray suit. She spotted him standing in the far corner of the room, holding a beer and talking to Zach. Their eyes met across the room. He said something to Zach and headed straight for her.

"Hi," he said warmly when he reached her side. "You look gorgeous." She glanced down at her lavender halter-style full-length dress. Not the most flattering style for her—being petite, it sort of swallowed up her body.

"Thanks, you too." He looked unbelievably handsome in a suit. Her mind flashed to their impromptu hookup the last time he'd worn a suit. So hot neither of them had thought of protection. She went up on tiptoe to whisper in his ear, "I'm not pregnant."

"I know," he said casually. "You told me it wouldn't happen."

"I thought I might hear from you."

"I knew I'd see you here."

She clenched her teeth, irritated with his casual attitude about what could've been a big deal.

"Was I supposed to call?" he asked.

"It's fine."

"Sorry. I thought you said it was okay, so—"

"Don't worry about it."

He fingered the tendril of hair that had been left down in her updo and spoke low near her ear. "I know enough to know that 'fine' and 'don't worry about it' means I screwed up. I might not always get it right, but I'll try."

She nodded, hating that she was so peeved, wishing for once she could be as laid-back and cool as men always were with her.

He tipped her chin up and kissed her. "You dancing with Ben?"

"Yeah. He's my match across the aisle."

"Who you dancing with after him?"

"Depends who asks."

He snaked an arm around her waist. "You're dancing with me."

She rested her hand on his chest, breathing in his clean woodsy scent, relaxing again. "I didn't hear you asking."

He leaned down to her ear. "Dance with me."

"Didn't hear a question mark in there."

He smiled one of his devastatingly handsome smiles. "Can you hear question marks?"

"Sure. Do you want to dance?" She lifted her voice at the end to show him.

"I'd love to."

"Hey! You tricked me into asking you."

He grinned and kissed her.

"Stop moving in on my dance partner, you horndog," Ben said, elbowing Ethan out of the way.

Ethan narrowed his eyes.

"I've got all the embarrassing stories on this guy." Ben grinned at Ally, his blue eyes twinkling mischievously. He bent his arm, offering it to her. "Hailey says we're supposed to join in now."

She took his arm and he led her onto the dance floor, where the rest of the bridal party was slowly gathering around Alex and Lauren. The photographer was circling them, taking pictures of all the pairings. She and Ben paused to smile for the camera.

"So you and Ethan, huh?" Ben asked, leading her in a waltz with enough space between them for polite manners.

"Nothing serious," Ally said. She was pretty sure Ethan wasn't serious. Otherwise, wouldn't he want to be in touch with her when they were apart? Didn't he think about her at all?

"You sure about that?" Ben asked.

"Uh, yeah. I think I would know."

"He's watching us like a hawk."

"He's just doing his cop thing, checking out the room."

"He's checking you out."

"He is not." She peeked over her shoulder. Ethan appeared to be looking at something in the distance. She turned back to Ben, who must've been teasing. "Ethan told me you and Logan are doing fantastic in your business."

"Yeah, business is good for Checkin. We're looking into getting some investors to expand even more."

"Why don't you just ask Jake for the investment?" Jake Campbell was rolling in it. He was already a wealthy tech CEO in his own right, and then he married Claire, who was wealthy on her own.

Ben grimaced. "Ever hear don't take money from family?"

"Yeah, but it's Jake." She wiggled her fingers at Jake, who smiled and turned so Claire could see her. Claire held up a finger to Ally and mouthed, "Hold on."

"Exactly," Ben said. "He's like a brother to me and I don't want to muck things up with money."

A few moments later, Claire and Jake were dancing next to them. "Ally, great news!" Claire exclaimed. "Misty Davies needs a second assistant."

Ally's stomach flipped. "Seriously?" Misty Davies was America's leading funny lady. Ally had always thought if they ever met, they'd immediately be best friends.

Claire smiled brightly. "Really! You interested? I'll text you her private number."

"Omigod! I can't believe this." She dropped her hold on Ben and shifted over to Claire, who was still slowly swaying with Jake. "Would it be in LA? What would I do?"

"You'd move with her wherever. She has a house in LA, but she spends most of her downtime at her house in Maui."

"Maui! I've never been to Hawaii!"

Claire smiled. "I know for sure she's heading to Rome next August for a remake of *Roman Holiday*."

"Rome," Ally said in awe.

"She really is a sweetheart," Claire said. "I think you'd get along with her great. She treats her staff like friends, but that doesn't mean you won't have to work hard. She's got a killer publicity machine going at all times, plus security is a must. You have to scout out every location before she arrives and coordinate with the rest of her staff. You'd be working with bodyguards, publicists, manager, agent, movie directors, producers, and press. Her personal makeup artist and hairdresser travel with her, along with her assistant, Hannah, and her two little Maltese doggies. You'd basically be joining the Misty entourage. Hannah is so overwhelmed she asked for an assistant. That's where you come in."

"Wow." She felt light-headed over this incredible opportunity.

The song ended and Claire gave her a hug. "Sleep on it, okay?"

"I love Misty. I feel like we could be best friends."

"Don't confuse the woman with the role. This will be more like looking behind the curtain. She's not going to be 'on' all the time. She's human."

"Thanks so much! I'll sleep on it, promise." Ally walked off the dance floor in a daze, her elation fading as she caught Ethan's eye from across the room. She didn't want to say goodbye to him. Maybe he could go with her and be a security guard for Misty. Or maybe she had a hard decision to make.

She halted in her tracks. Ethan strode confidently toward her, his expression serious, his naturally tough demeanor bringing an air of authority. Except she knew him differently, knew he took care with her, even if it was in a gruff way. His intense gaze was locked on her, and the closer he got to her, the more her body reacted, her skin flushing with heat, her pulse thrumming faster, her mouth dry.

He stopped in front of her abruptly. "What happened? You look shell-shocked."

She blinked up at him. "Claire just offered me the most amazing opportunity. She says Misty Davies—you know who that is, right?"

"Yeah, everyone knows her."

"Well, her assistant needs an assistant. Claire recommended me. I could be part of the Misty entourage, traveling to LA, Maui, Rome, and who knows where else. I can hardly believe it."

Ethan frowned. "You want to be an assistant to an assistant to a movie star?"

"It's Rome! I've never been to Rome. Even better, I'll get to see movie sets, all the exclusive areas that only movie stars can go like VIP rooms of clubs, private rooms of restaurants, penthouse suites. This is the glam exciting opportunity I was hoping for."

He took her hand. "Come on, let's talk somewhere private."

She swallowed hard and followed him out of the ballroom. If Ethan wanted to have a serious talk, if he told her that he loved her, she'd stay. She knew she would. Love was a precious fragile thing and she didn't ever take it for granted when it happened. But if he didn't love her, if he just liked her a lot and enjoyed their weekend hookups, well, then, she'd have to say goodbye.

He led her to an empty parlor, where they sat in two red velvet cushioned chairs. He shifted to face her. "I know movie star stuff sounds exciting, but it's work."

"You don't understand. For Hollywood, work and fun are mixed together."

He let out a long breath. "I guess."

"You don't approve."

He hesitated before saying, "Is this what would make you happy? Is this your true purpose?"

"It's an adventure. Maybe you could come with me? Like as part of her security detail?"

He shook his head. "I didn't become a cop to follow around some actress. And I've put in a lot of years with Eastman PD. I'm not that far from retiring with a full pension."

"Retiring? You're not that old."

"Cops can retire after putting in twenty years." His gaze was intense. "Besides, everything I need is right here."

"Do you not want me to take the job?" She held her breath. Now she'd know where she really stood with him.

He clenched his jaw before saying in a low voice, "I'd never stand in your way, Ally. I want you to be happy."

Her heart sank. Why had she hoped for a declaration of love? Why did she get her hopes up like this every time? She always read too much into her relationships.

"Claire told me to sleep on it," Ally said. "So I will, but Misty needs someone right away."

"For how long?"

"I don't know."

They were quiet for a few moments. She took in his

serious expression and gave it one last try because she had to be sure about him before she made her decision.

She leaned close. "Eth," she whispered, "how do you really feel about us? About me."

"I like you." He nodded once. "A lot. I like you a lot."

"I love you," she blurted.

He jerked straight up in his seat and stared at her like she'd grown a third head. Maybe he was in shock. Maybe she'd held back so much before that he hadn't realized how much he meant to her.

"I love you, Ethan," she said again through the tightness in her throat.

Still no response.

Because he didn't feel the same way.

She stood on shaky legs, her heart sinking to the pit of her stomach. "Okay. I'm going to go now."

He remained still and silent.

She headed back toward the ballroom, needing the comfort of her friends, nausea rising in her throat. Ethan was just like every other guy she'd gotten involved with; they never cared about her as much as she cared about them. Or maybe they were all just closed off, emotionally stunted. What did that say about her that she seemed to find this kind of guy?

She took one step into the ballroom, took in all the happy couples, and made a beeline for the ladies' room, where she promptly threw up.

So much for single me, happy me. Nothing with men had ever been easy for her.

15

Ethan punched the living room wall and then shook his sore knuckles. Dammit. Ally had just texted that she took the stupid movie star assistant opportunity. The woman was true to her word. She said she'd sleep on it and literally the very next day she made her decision. She was hoping to leave in two weeks. He should've told her he loved her, but he'd choked. He couldn't get the words out. Why couldn't he say it? His whole life he'd been waiting for someone to say it to him, she finally did, and he'd gone numb. Something in him just shut down. What the hell was wrong with him?

His phone rang and he snatched it up, ridiculously hopeful that it was Ally. Nope. Joe, his honorary dad.

"Hey, what's up?" Ethan said curtly.

"I've got some news."

Ethan straightened, immediately on alert. "What happened? Is everything okay?"

"Everything's fine. I wanted to let you know Peggy's estate is going to you and Zach. She left you everything."

Joe's voice reached him through a long tunnel. His foster mom left him everything? He could barely comprehend.

"Eth?"

"What estate? Why me and Zach? Why am I just hearing about this now? Peggy died two months ago."

"It takes a while for these things to go through. She made me executor of her will. It had to have a court hearing first. We were waiting to hear if any kin might object to the will. No one came forward. Now it's official. Her house and everything in it are yours."

He stared at the floor, his vision blurry. Why would she leave it to him?

Joe went on. "I've been looking in on the house once a week. It's in good shape. Zach stopped by this morning and I gave him the key. He's waiting to hear from you about going over there."

Ethan jerked his head up. "Yeah, okay. Bye." He hung up and called Zach.

"Guess you heard," Zach said.

"You got some time to go over there?" It was Sunday, so they both had the day off.

"Yeah, I'm home. I'll meet you there in ten."

Ethan drove over in case he needed to haul something away, though he could've walked, he lived just on the other side of town. He beat Zach there and parked in front of the three-bedroom ranch house that had been his first real home. The white vinyl siding and black shutters were in good condition, the yard full of leaves again. He'd just raked them a couple of weeks ago. His heart lodged in his throat. He could just see Peggy out here in her old brown coat and sensible brown shoes, raking the leaves like she did every fall. She was a no-nonsense practical woman. Strong. She must've been so strong to build a life on her own, a widow who'd lost her only son and then went on to foster so many kids well after the age most people retired.

He made his way to the backyard, grabbed the rake leaning against the back of the house, and got to work, his mind wandering back to Peggy's death right in this yard. She'd died under the heat of the late August sun, pulling weeds in her flower beds. Eighty-four years old and her heart just gave out. Unfortunately, since she'd been in the backyard when she collapsed, her neighbor hadn't noticed until it was too late to revive her.

Guilt stabbed at him and he raked harder, long sweeping strokes. He hadn't seen Peggy since his birthday back in June. She'd made him his favorite dessert, carrot cake. He gave her a gift card to her favorite store, Target, like he always did when he visited. Now it seemed so impersonal. They hadn't hugged.

He stopped, leaning on the rake, lost in memories of this house and Peggy.

"Eth!"

He snapped to attention at Zach's appearance. His foster brother was his age, tall and lean with dark brown hair on the shaggy side and a full beard that probably fit in perfectly with his job as a professor. "Hey."

"Ready?"

His knees locked. It was never going to be easy to go through Peggy's things. He hadn't been inside the house since his birthday. "Sure." He set the rake back against the side of the house and followed Zach to the front door.

"Did you know Joe was the executor of her will?" Zach asked.

"No, but I'm not too surprised. Joe was her emergency person. They were in touch a lot when we were kids." Peggy had thought it important that he and Zach have a male role model and encouraged them to spend as much time as they wanted with the Campbells. With all the boys close to their age hanging around the Campbell house, that meant they spent nearly all of their free time there. Peggy's house became a place to sleep and eat. She was brisk and efficient, the place was always clean, homemade meals on the table. His gut churned. He'd taken her for granted. She had nobody. Her husband long ago passed, her son killed by a drunk driver. Why hadn't he visited more? He hadn't realized how much he meant to her.

"True." Zach pulled the key out of his jeans pocket, stuck it in the lock, and blew out a breath.

Ethan reached out and finished the job, opening the front door. Neither of them moved.

"Why did she leave everything to us?" Ethan asked.

"There was a constant parade of foster kids through this house before and after us. I don't get it."

Zach turned to face him. "She loved us the most."

"Bullshit. She didn't love us. She never said she loved us. I can't remember even a hug from her."

Zach's light brown eyes met his, sad and sympathetic. "She wasn't an affectionate woman, but that doesn't mean she didn't love us. She took good care of us, gave us a stable drama-free home. She worked with Joe to make sure we had a father figure." Zach's voice choked and he pinched the bridge of his nose.

A weight pressed on Ethan's chest, the tension unbearable. He stepped around Zach and into the house, barely seeing it. Regret hammered him. She had no family. He and Zach were both orphans. Was that why she loved them? Because they were the same? Alone.

He looked around at the same furniture from when he'd lived there—beige sofa, brown high-back chair, simple wooden coffee table and matching end tables. A tall standing lamp next to the chair for reading. No decorations, no framed pictures. Austere, neat, no sentimentality. Just like Peggy.

"It never changed," Zach murmured, joining him in the center of the room.

"I always had this weird sense of déjà vu when I visited. Like any minute you were going to walk out of the kitchen nine years old again."

"Yeah."

They took a tour of the place. It was a modest space. He and Zach had probably stayed the longest. There were always two or three more kids rotating through, a lot of siblings that stuck close together. Most of them went back to their parents or other family.

Zach went into their old room and sat on the twin bed that used to be his.

Ethan remained standing, his mind a jumble of old memories. "If she loved us so much, why didn't she adopt us?"

Zach shook his head. "I don't know. Maybe she tried, but there was some bias against her because she was single. They didn't do many single-parent adoptions back then. Maybe she needed the money the foster care system sent for us." He lifted his palms. "Does it really matter now?"

It shouldn't, but it did. He shoved his hands in his pockets and turned away. It would've made a huge difference to him to know he was loved, to know he was good enough to be adopted. Zach already had that. He remembered his mom loved him before she was killed. Ethan had no memories to fall back on.

He headed over to the hallway and peeked into the other small bedroom. Bunk beds and a twin bed. Wood dresser and nightstand. Neat and empty. Then he went to Peggy's room. He'd never spent any time in here, just peeked in once in a while as a kid. It was just as plain as the rest of the house. A queen-size bed with an oak headboard and a light blue comforter. The long dresser and two nightstands were matching oak. There was only one bathroom in the house, out in the hallway. Geez, what had that been like for her to share a bathroom with two teenaged boys and a parade of other kids? He'd never thought about it before.

He opened a nightstand drawer and found a small spiral notebook and pen. He closed the drawer again and gingerly sat on the side of the bed. It smelled like her in here, clean like fresh soap and lemon Pledge.

Zach came in and looked around.

"There's a notebook in the nightstand," Ethan said.

Zach pulled it out and opened it, showing Ethan with a small smile. "Grocery lists and menus. She probably used these when she was still fostering."

Ethan took a look, recognizing one of the meals he'd had, meatloaf and homemade mac 'n cheese.

Zach looked through a small closet with a rack of house-dresses and a few nicer dresses she'd worn to church. Shoes lined up at the bottom, sweaters neatly folded on the top shelf. Ethan stood and paced the room.

Zach started poking through the dresser drawers. He stopped at the bottom drawer and pulled out a large envelope. He carefully pulled the contents out and laid them on top of the dresser. "Eth."

"I feel weird looking at her stuff."

"It's us."

The weight on his chest made it hard to breathe. Zach was spreading out some pictures. How could he not have known he was special to her? He made his way over to Zach and stared in shock. Individual wallet-size school pictures of him and Zach, every grade, along with pictures of each of them on their birthday, every year from nine to eighteen, and then Ethan and Zach together at their high school graduation in cap and gown, grinning at the camera. Zach was valedictorian with a ton of honors. Ethan was not.

The kid pictures of him and Zach were a study in contrasts. There was Zach, staring back at the camera with solid confidence, knowing he was smart because he got straight As, knowing he was loved because he remembered his mom. And then Ethan, the lost little boy, then angry, then teenaged sneering.

"Her husband," Zach said, setting more pictures out. There was a man in a Marine uniform and their wedding pictures. Peggy looked completely different as a bride. Her hair was dark brown and past her shoulders; she had round cheeks like she still had some baby fat. She'd always looked thin when he'd known her, and her hair had been short and gray. He looked on the back for the year and showed Zach.

"Child bride," Zach commented. "Eighteen."

"You think she was pregnant?"

"People got married younger back then. Maybe her husband was stationed overseas and it was easier to get married."

There were a lot of pictures of her son. He flipped to the back of one, where her neat print said: Michael, one year, five months. He'd been born a couple of years after the wedding. The pictures stopped abruptly at age nine.

"That's when he died," Ethan said. And he'd been close to that age when he arrived here.

"Yeah. She told me about it once. He was riding his bike in

the early morning and a drunk driver hit him. It was a teenager on an all-night bender."

He swore under his breath. "I didn't know all that."

"She told me stuff sometimes. I think it was because I was so quiet sitting there at the kitchen table long after everyone else was done eating."

"You were always so slow." He pushed down the stab of jealousy. Peggy had never confided in Ethan.

"I was usually thinking," Zach said. "Some people talk more because the silence makes them uncomfortable. She probably would've told you stuff if you'd sat there long enough." He held up a small white envelope. "Sealed."

"Maybe it's from her husband."

Zach handed it to him. "No address. You open it."

Ethan's stomach rolled. "It's private. Just put it back."

"We're her kin. No one else is ever going to see this stuff. We have to decide what to do with it. Maybe this will tell us what she wants."

"Then you open it."

"I did the pictures. You think that was easy?"

He studied Zach for a moment. His face was pinched, tight with tension. "You sounded normal."

"I was looking at it intellectually like an anthropologist. Letter is more personal. Please, Eth. Can you take this one?" Zach walked over to the bed and sat down.

"Fine," he grumbled. Zach had that luxury, hiding in his head because he was an academic. Ethan didn't work that way, he felt everything in his body. He carefully opened it and pulled out a neatly folded piece of lined paper. He unfolded it and began to read, her neat handwriting at once bringing back memories. She would leave little notes for them some-times, like if they got home too late for dinner, just simple stuff like "meatloaf in the fridge."

"Read it out loud," Zach said.

Ethan swallowed hard. "Dear Ethan and Zach, you are my greatest success story. I'm so proud of how you became like brothers and helped each other to be the best you could be. It was my—" Ethan's voice choked and he looked to the ceiling for a moment, fighting back tears. He cleared his throat and continued. "It was my privilege to watch you turn into the great men you are today. Ethan with your outstanding service as a police officer, and Zach out there teaching people about people."

Zach's voice held a note of amusement. "She never did understand my job as an anthropologist."

"Can you blame her? It's not like a lot of people around here do what you do."

"Guess not. Keep going."

Ethan took a deep breath. "You're my family now, so I'm leaving you the house and everything in it. Joe has all the legal particulars. I was glad to be a safe place for you to land if only for a short portion of your life. I have one thing of value hidden in the oatmeal container in the back of the kitchen cabinet. It's my engagement ring, an antique twin marquis diamond ring from my husband's mother. Maybe one of you would like to carry on the tradition and give it to a woman one day, or maybe you'd each like a diamond to set in a new ring. I'll leave it to you to work out the details. Love, Peggy."

Ethan stared at the letter for a moment before lifting his head to an empty room. He set the letter down on the dresser and headed over to the kitchen, where Zach was digging through some of the high cabinets. Ethan thought for a moment. Where would Peggy hide her only treasure?

He squatted down and opened the largest lower cabinet Peggy used like a small pantry for items she used infrequently. And there it was—behind the flour, sugar, Bisquick, and a Ziplocked bag of raisin bran. He retrieved the oatmeal container and opened it. Oatmeal. *Dig deeper.* He shoved his hand in, and there at the bottom was a plastic bag. He pulled it out. A Ziploc sandwich bag with a diamond ring inside.

He straightened and took out the ring, holding it up and looking at it from all angles. It was unusual—two marquis-cut diamonds sat at an angle nestled by smaller chips of diamonds on a gold band.

"Found it," he muttered.

Zach shut a cabinet and crossed to him. "Wow. They don't make them like this anymore."

Ethan offered it to him. "Here. You're into old stuff."

"I already gave Carrie an engagement ring. It's your turn."

"I'm not getting married."

"You will."

"How do you know?"

"I've seen the way you look at Ally."

Ethan clenched his jaw. He'd already screwed things up permanently with Ally. Now she was leaving.

Zach shoved his shoulder. "Peggy's giving you the look from heaven right now."

He reluctantly smiled. Peggy never raised her voice. When she was displeased, she'd just shoot you this quelling look that made you stand up straighter. He carefully put the ring back in the plastic bag and stuck it in his pocket.

Zach put his hands on his hips and looked around. "You want this place?"

Ethan considered. "No. It's too much her."

"Yeah, I get that. I want Carrie to pick the house she wants. So we agreed on selling? Split the profits?"

"Yeah. We can run an estate sale for the furniture, donate whatever's left."

"I think Peggy would be okay with that. She'd want us to have a good start for our own homes." He rubbed his beard. "I'll take the pictures of me, you take the pictures of you."

Ethan nodded. "What about the pictures of her husband and son?"

"We'll divvy them up." Zach clasped his hand and then pulled him in for a hug.

Ethan, who normally wouldn't hug his brother more than a quick around-the-neck squeeze, returned the hug, wrapping his arms around Zach and clapping him on the back. "She made us a family and I didn't know it until now."

Zach pulled back and gave him a watery smile. "She loved us."

"Yeah," he choked out. "She did." And he felt that all the way through, the knowledge warming him, making his heart open, his chest expanding like he could breathe a full breath for the first time in his life. Like he was a new man. One who'd been wanted and loved as a kid.

Zach squeezed Ethan's shoulder. "I'll gather up the stuff in the envelope and we'll go."

Ethan nodded and just stood there alone in the kitchen, memories of Peggy cooking and serving up dinner flooding him. He could practically taste his favorite mac 'n cheese. Peggy washing dishes in her apron with the little red ruffle around the edges. The rectangular Formica table full of kids, talking and shoveling in food, Peggy quietly presiding at one end of it. He hadn't been paying attention. Hadn't noticed the love she showed through her actions, her quiet patience, her competent care. She'd given him the foundation he'd needed. She'd given him love. He'd been longing for what he'd had all along.

Her death had been a wake-up call, making him try to be more open, but he hadn't quite gotten there. He'd frozen up when Ally had said she loved him. And what about everyone else? Peggy, Joe, his honorary brothers and sister.

His heart thundered in his chest. "I love you, Peggy," he whispered, the words strange on his tongue. A rush of warmth ran through him. For a moment he swore he felt the soft touch of a hand on his back.

Zach appeared in the living room with the envelope. "Ready?"

He swallowed hard. "L—" He coughed, his cheeks burning, but he forced the words out anyway. "Love you, bro."

Zach smiled widely. "Love you too."

Ethan nodded once, patted the ring in his pocket, and followed Zach out the door with a lightness in his step.

16

———

Ethan finished raking Peggy's yard, drove home, tucked the ring and pictures in a drawer, and then walked right back out, too keyed up to be confined. Instead he walked across town to Joe's house. He needed to talk to him about Peggy.

Joe answered the door with a sympathetic look. "Thought it would be you. Zach coming too?"

"No, he's too hooked on Carrie to leave her for long."

Joe clapped him on the shoulder. "You want a drink?"

"Sure." They often sat around the kitchen table, having a drink and talking. As a kid, it was water, milk or, for big talks, something more enticing like lemonade. Nowadays, it was beer.

He sat at the table and waited for Joe to join him with the beers. They clinked bottles and each took a sip.

Joe let out a breath. "You made her proud. She always told me that."

"You guys talk about me a lot?"

"We had regular talks about you and Zach. She considered me a partner in raising you. She'd say, who needs a village to raise a child when the Campbell family is just a few blocks away?"

Ethan picked at the label on his beer bottle. "I should've visited her more. I can't believe she left me and Zach everything. I thought we were just two of a long line of kids passing through."

"Peggy wasn't the kind to gush over someone. She showed them her love by taking care of them."

Ethan took a pull on his beer, desperate to loosen up the tight ball of regret lodged there. He met Joe's kind brown eyes, the only dad he'd ever known and a damn good one at that. His role model. He'd become a cop because of Joe. He wanted to say the words for him too. He should've said them long ago. He cleared his throat, but the words still came out on a croak, "I love you, Dad." He'd never called him dad out loud before either. It felt right.

His dad smiled, the lines around his eyes crinkling. "I love you too, Ethan."

His heart thundered at the words he'd waited his whole life to hear and now he'd heard them several times over. He rubbed his knuckles over the wetness in his eyes. How had he not known deep down that he had love in his life? And why couldn't he say it for so long?

His dad squeezed his shoulder. "You've been family since the first time you sneered at me at eight years old. I saw through that tough veneer to the good heart underneath."

"No one adopted me." He hated that it still mattered. Why hadn't they? Why hadn't Peggy? He could understand Joe not adopting him. He was a single dad with six kids plus Parker. There were so many kids at the Campbell house, Joe could barely fit them all, everyone doubling up with bunk beds, Parker on the sofa.

"Eth, Peggy wanted to. She tried to adopt you and Zach. She wanted you to stay together, but Social Services wasn't keen on letting single women adopt back then and they were also concerned about her age. She was sixty when she applied."

Ethan's mind whirled. "What? Why didn't anyone tell me?"

"She didn't want to get your hopes up if it didn't work out."

"But I would've wanted to know. Does Zach know?"

His dad shook his head. "You guys were ten. It was a judgment call. She pleaded her case with Social Services, and they decided not to pursue other adoptive parents for you guys. She could be your foster mom as long as she was in good health. It was an unofficial adoption."

Ethan clenched his jaw. He could've been adopted for real or at least known Peggy wanted him enough to try. How much time and energy had he wasted being angry at the world for not being wanted? And Peggy lived to be eighty-four. She definitely could've been his adoptive mom. What kind of system turns away a perfectly capable woman from making a family?

His dad interrupted his dark thoughts. "I think you and Zach were meant to go to her. She gave you a stable foundation; we gave you the crazy family. I'd say you turned out okay. And, Eth, you made everyone so proud with your work, all your commendations, and how you've been there for all your brothers and little sister."

Ethan rubbed his forehead and closed his eyes. "Today was the first time I've ever said I love you to anyone."

"What's been stopping you?"

He opened his eyes, the truth painful to admit. "I don't know."

His dad socked him on the shoulder. "We all know you love us; otherwise you wouldn't keep hanging around."

He laughed a little. "Yeah."

The doorbell rang and his dad went to answer it. Ethan pulled out his phone and texted Zach about Peggy trying to adopt them and being turned down. Zach texted back a moment later. *All good. End result was the same.*

Obviously Zach didn't have adoption hang-ups like Ethan did. Ethan stood and headed toward the happy noise of two-year-old Viv in the living room. Her parents, Alex and Lauren, were probably dropping off Viv before they left for their honeymoon, a short couple of days away to the Finger Lakes of New York.

Ethan couldn't help but smile at little Viv. She certainly had her own unique style. She wore her beloved Frankenstein mask with her pigtails sticking out the top, with a Wonder Woman outfit complete with gold wristbands. Halloween was on Thursday.

"Wow," Ethan said. "Awesome costume, Viv."

She growled at him and then ran one length of the room to the other, her red cape flying out behind her.

"Hey, Eth," Alex said. His honorary brother was three years younger and a good man. A great dad to Viv too.

Ethan's chest ached and he walked right over and hugged Alex, who stiffened and then clapped him on the back. "Love you, bro," Ethan croaked.

Alex's eyes were wide. "Ah…I love you too."

Viv ran over and clung to Alex's leg. Ethan bent down, the words coming easier now. "I love you, scary Wonder Woman."

"Love you, Efan," she said in the sweetest voice.

His hand went to his heart. He straightened and met Lauren's kind eyes. "She got me."

Lauren hugged him, enveloping him in soft feminine affection. "We all love you, Eth."

"Enough hugging," Alex barked when the hug went on too long for him.

Ethan pulled away from Lauren and wiped his eyes. Anyone would be worked up after finding out their foster mom had adopted them in spirit. Peggy was his mom in every way that counted.

"What's with all the mushy stuff?" Alex asked.

His dad answered for him. "He and Zach just went through Peggy's things. She left them everything. And Ethan just realized how much she loved them."

Alex bowed his head. "She was a good woman."

Fuck, he was gonna lose it. His throat constricted, his eyes hot. "I gotta go."

He left, walking at a brisk pace and then running. He took to heart the hard lesson he'd learned today. He would tell the people in his life that he loved them, and that included Ally. Would it make a difference? Would she want to stay to build a life with him?

When he got home, he pulled the antique engagement ring from the drawer and stared at it. Did he want a committed future with Ally because he wanted to get married now or just to keep her from leaving?

If he hadn't been given this ring, would he have proposed?

He closed his eyes. *Yes.* He wanted a home with Ally, a family of his own, his blood.

His plan was simple. Tell Ally he loved her. Propose.

He had everything he needed now.

He just had to reach out and take it.

Ethan wanted to tell Ally the love words in person, but he had to wait. No choice but to wait because he broke down, a delayed response to grief and loss. Honestly, he was a complete wreck for three whole days and had to take the week off work. He'd never grieved his parents, couldn't remember them, and some part of him had held back really grieving Peggy. Maybe his heart hadn't been ready despite his intellectual decision back when she'd first died to be more open. Now he knew what it felt like to really have an open heart, every emotion so much more intense.

Today he and Zach had met with a real estate agent about selling the house and then cleared it out. That had helped, actually, because once they finished, Zach held an impromptu memorial service, where they each shared their memories of Peggy and said goodbye. She hadn't wanted a funeral, so he'd never really said goodbye before. Today's simple ceremony with Zach had been so much better.

Now he was feeling more like his old self again, only better. He showed up at Garner's that night for the Halloween costume party, bursting with his newfound capacity for love. He was a little late because he'd left Thor's hammer back at his place and didn't realize it until he'd parked, and he had to go back and get it. Without the hammer, he just looked like a muscled guy with a red cape and boots with a long blond wig. At least it was sleeveless, so he could show he had the real muscles under the padded muscle chest top.

"Thor!" the guys hollered. The women weren't here yet. Probably still getting ready.

He bounded forward and swung his hammer. "Fortunately, I am mighty," he said, quoting the movie.

The guys laughed. Zach snatched his hammer and twirled it around.

He approached the bar, where Josh, the bartender and his honorary brother, stood dressed in a black hat and eye mask. "Who're you supposed to be? Zorro?"

"Lone Ranger."

"Clarissa your Tonto?" Ethan quipped.

Josh responded in a serious tone. "No, she's an angel. Fitting, I guess. She's a good person." Josh blew out a breath. "Really good."

"Too good for you," Ethan joked, not sure what the problem was.

"Yeah," Josh said halfheartedly, seeming lost in thought.

Ethan tapped the bar, and Josh snapped to attention. "Mead, please, and I love you, bro."

Josh's jaw dropped. "Are you dying, man?"

"No."

Logan, the youngest Campbell brother, approached and elbowed Ethan in the gut. "Move over, Thor."

"Love you, bro," Ethan said. He was on a mission. Every single brother had to know. Four down—Zach, Alex, Josh, Logan—five to go. And his "little sister" Mad too.

"What's with all this love shit?" Josh asked.

"You taking estrogen or something?" Logan asked with a smirk.

Sarcastic bastards.

"This is why I never said this shit before," Ethan barked. "Fuck you all. I learned my lesson with Peggy and now I love every single frigging one of you. Deal with it."

The guys went silent. Everyone knew what he'd lost. And then someone said, "Well, shit."

Then they were crowding him, pounding him on the back, knocking into his shoulder. Someone mussed his hair. Josh reached across the bar and gave his cheek a slap.

And he knew they all loved him back.

~

Ally walked in to the Halloween party to a strange sight. All the guys were piling on Ethan, jostling him and messing up his wig while he grinned like the hottest Thor she'd ever seen and that included the movie version.

She rushed into the fray with a classic line. "You are no match for the mighty Thor!"

The guys parted, making room for her.

"Ally," Ethan said, serious now. He pulled her tight against his massively muscled chest made even more so with padded muscles.

She hugged him back. She'd missed him. She hadn't seen him since Lauren's wedding. Lauren had told her about Ethan inheriting his foster mom's estate and how hard he'd taken it, so Ally had called him, but their conversation had been short. He'd explained he needed some time to grieve, but he wanted to talk to her face-to-face here with all their friends because he had "serious shit to say to everyone." She'd been cautiously optimistic that he might say he wanted to go with her on her new job adventure or that he really didn't want her to go after all. She hadn't given notice at work yet. Ethan's serious talk had sounded important enough to put her plans on hold. Temporarily.

He spoke near her ear. "I'm so glad you're here."

"Me too. You doing okay?" She hadn't been overly worried about him because she knew Zach was with him a lot, the brothers leaning on each other as they said goodbye to their foster mom. Carrie had kept her updated.

He nodded. "Yeah. I'm doing a lot better." He pulled back, seeming to notice her costume for the first time. "You look like you belong with Thor. What is this sexy thing you've got on?"

She beamed. "I'm a goddess." The costume was a white maxi dress with side slits that showed lots of skin on her torso and from upper thigh to ankle. Gold accents made it shine with a gold headband, gold choker necklace, gold belt, and gold bracelets.

"Yeah, you are." He pushed his long flowing blond hair over his shoulder; then he took her hand and led her to a quiet corner of the room. He stopped and framed her face with his hands, gazing deep into her eyes. "I love you, Ally."

She slapped a hand over her mouth, her eyes filling.

He pulled her hand from her mouth and held it in a warm clasp. "I'm sorry I didn't say it before. I felt it, but something in me just shut down. No one's ever said it to me before and it made me feel unworthy somehow, but then I started saying it and people started saying it back."

"What people?" she blurted. "You're just saying this to everyone?"

"No! Not at all. I told my dad. My brothers. Family. I love you different than that." He shifted and his hammer bounced off her leg. "Sorry." He set it back on the bar and Logan started playing with it, bopping Ben on the head.

He returned to her, taking both her hands in his. "I don't want you to go to LA or Maui or Rome. At least not with that movie star. I'll take you wherever you want to go, but in the meantime, I want you to stay here with me because I love you." His voice was rough with emotion, making her heart thump hard and her eyes well. "I want to build a life with you."

"Eth," she choked out over the lump in her throat.

He lifted a hand, gently stroking her hair back from her face, his eyes searching hers.

"Yes!" she exclaimed, an electric surge of love lighting her up inside. She threw herself in his arms and kissed him all over his gorgeous face. "I love you too! I'll stay for love. I'll stay for you."

He closed his eyes for a moment, murmuring, "Thank you." Then he smiled tenderly, cradled her jaw, and kissed her. "Are you sure? Be sure. I don't want to hold you back."

"Love is worth more than any VIP first-class ticket."

He wrapped his arms around her in a tight hug before pulling back just enough to kiss her. She kissed him back passionately with all the love in her heart. Nothing had ever felt more right. She chose love and she'd never been happier.

"Thor and the goddess are making out," someone said. "Get a picture."

17

It was a joyous Saturday night Happy Endings Book Club meeting at the private hotel lounge in the city. The first time since the sologamy ceremony that they'd been able to have a book club meeting with Claire. Ally marveled over the month that had passed since marrying herself. In hindsight, she'd thrown herself into sologamy with just as much blind enthusiasm as she had her old sappy romantic fantasy life, but sologamy turned out to be a good way of healing and moving forward. She'd accomplished a lot, reaching out for new experiences like her fitness classes and hiking and fishing and, finally, taking the risk of letting a man into her life. Not just any man, the best man she'd ever met. Ethan had never once tried to hold her back while she'd searched for what would make her truly content. He'd just been supportive and kind and loving. He was better than any prince she could've imagined. She was sure her friends thought she was a lovesick dope, but ever since Ethan openly returned her love, she'd been floating, all gooey and giddy over absolutely everything.

Ally looked around the circle of women with a goofy smile, glad she wouldn't have to say goodbye to them anytime soon. Now that she was staying local, she was looking for a bigger career opportunity than an assistant job, something she could really help build. She was still thinking on what. Tonight they were supposed to be talking about *The Princess Bride*, an impossibly romantic fairy tale that had once been Ally's favorite fantasy. Everyone was wearing the Dread Pirate Roberts T-shirt Claire had given them at her wedding as her promise that she'd be back to talk about the book and then watch the movie together.

But like usual, the meeting got off track. The discussion started with *The Princess Bride*, but then quickly veered to the personal—how beautiful Lauren's wedding had been last Saturday, which led to Carrie sharing some of the planning she was already doing with Hailey and the *Bride Special* magazine people for her own wedding next June.

Ally chimed in. "If only sologamy ceremonies could get so much attention, right? It would probably help so many women feel good about themselves."

Sabrina agreed. "If you came up with something, I'd be happy to share it with my clients struggling with singlehood."

"Maybe I could make special kits with vows and a necklace," Ally said, thinking out loud.

"Or you could make it a bachelorette party thing," Lauren chimed in.

Missy huffed. "For the last time, women want strippers at their bachelorette party."

They cracked up.

"Get the woman a stripper!" Mad exclaimed, which set them off again.

Once everyone quieted, Ally returned to the sologamy idea, hope sparking within her. "You really think there's a market for sologamy stuff?"

"Absolutely," Missy said with a nod. "I think it's a worthy cause."

"Wow," Ally muttered. "I never really thought about it before, but I have been looking for a new business venture."

Hailey leaned across the circle toward Ally, her brows shooting up, a wide smile lighting up her face. Not her stressed-out beauty-queen smile either, more of a super-excited smile. "Really?"

Ally exchanged a look of concern with her friends. Ever since Josh and Clarissa had gotten together three weeks ago, Hailey had been a little…hyper. It was the first weekend in November, which meant everything had slowed down for Hailey's wedding planning business, but Hailey had sped up, throwing herself into community events. So far she'd arranged a massive Black Friday shop-local campaign for Clover Park, a holiday stroll for the following weekend, including not just the usual decorations and breakfast with Santa, but also an ice-sculpture artist, strolling carolers, horse and carriage rides down Main Street, an outdoor crafters market under a heated tent, and a hot cocoa station with glazed nuts. She had more in the works too, some kind of holiday fundraising event at Ludbury House to benefit a local food bank and Toys for Tots, as well as something special for senior citizens she was still thinking on. It made Ally tired just hearing about it all.

Ally spoke slowly and cautiously. "Yeah, I'd like something I could help build."

"Ally!" Hailey squealed, wiggling in her seat. "That sologamy thing could be a nice add-on to my business! I could put it on my website as an option." She gestured wildly. "You could guide the bride and bridesmaids through their own special ceremony to make them feel empowered and good about themselves. Like you did with us!" She looked to their friends for confirmation, who quickly agreed.

Ally considered it. The idea had merit and she was sure once Hailey was back to her usual non-hyper self, she'd be good to work with. "I have been looking to get out of the classroom, just get out there and do something awesome." A slow smile dawned. "This could be *really* awesome."

Hailey bounced in her seat. "Yes! Come work for me! I'm going to need someone very soon. You can be my right-hand woman and run the sologamy service. I can train you on weekends until the school year's over. Once that *Bride Special* article comes out next August, it's going to be nuts. Then I could bring you on full time. It's perfect!"

Ally wiggled in her seat. "Omigod, it is perfect! I *love* that idea!"

Hailey leapt out of her seat and Ally met her halfway for a jumping hug.

"What's all the hugging about?" a familiar masculine voice asked.

Ally startled. She pulled away to see Ethan heading straight for her. The guys were right on his heels.

Claire stood. "I invited the guys here for drinks. I know you usually have after book club meeting drinks, so I thought we'd just shift it here so I could join in. Hope that's okay with you all." She squeaked as her husband came up behind her and goosed her. Then he wrapped his arms around her from behind and nuzzled her neck.

"Absolutely," was the general consensus. At least from the women reuniting with their husbands and fiancés. The single women eyed the single men, who all headed over to the fully stocked bar, where Marcus and Josh immediately got to work serving up drinks. Marcus owned his own bar, The Burrow, a popular place in lower Manhattan. Luckily Josh hadn't brought his new girlfriend; otherwise Hailey might've shifted from hyper to manic and who knew what she'd plan then? Maybe a statewide dance marathon or a bare-chested bachelor auction. Actually, a bachelor auction could be fun. Ally smiled to herself, already shifting to planning mode. This new business opportunity was definitely a good fit for her.

Ally shared the good news with Ethan right after he gave her a big kiss. "I've got a fantastic job opportunity! I'm going to be working with Hailey, helping with wedding planning and offering sologamy ceremonies so everyone can feel happily empowered."

He gave her one of his rare big smiles that lit up his gorgeous face. "Awesome. I love it and I love you." He was so expressive now like his heart had cracked open and the love just poured out.

She melted, heart squeezing, weak in the knees, goofy smile and all. "Oh, Eth! I love you too."

He snagged her by the hips. "Maybe one day you'll be planning one of those weddings for us."

"You asking?"

"I will." He looked around at the noisy crowd and back to her. "Not here. I want to do it right. Would you like that one day with me? Something permanent?"

She nodded happily. "I would."

He entwined his fingers with hers, lifted her hand, and kissed her fingers. "I would too. I could not love you any more than I do in this moment."

"Aww," Ally exclaimed, her heart bursting with happiness. "Me too!"

"More lovey-dovey stuff, Eth? Give it a rest." Ben appeared at Ethan's side and elbowed him. Ethan just grinned.

Missy crossed to Ally. "Hey, leave them alone," she told Ben. "If they want to be lovey bears, more power to them." She fist-bumped Ally.

Ben stared at Missy. "Do I know you?"

Missy rolled her eyes. "We played pool together, like, four months ago." At Ben's confused look, she added, "At Marcus's bar? That mixer Hailey planned. Ring any bells?"

Ben's brows scrunched together in confusion. "We played pool together?"

"Yeah, on the same team." At his continued confusion, she added, "I could *not* be less flattered right now."

Ben barked out a laugh. "I'm sorry." He studied her for a moment. "Wait, did you used to have red hair?"

"Yeah, it's naturally red, but I dyed it dark brown. My face is the same."

"I never remember a face," he joked, his blue eyes glinting mischievously. He glanced down at her body and then met her eyes, giving her his usual charming dimpled smile. "I do remember you! Missy Higgins." He offered his hand. "Ben Wright."

"I remember *you*, Mr. *Wrong*." She laughed dryly and walked away. Ben's gaze followed her.

Ally bit back a smile. Mr. Wright had sure been wrong tonight.

"Mr. Wrong." Ethan chuckled. "She got that right."

"Oh, shut up, lovey bear." Ben stalked off to the other guys.

Ally smiled, shaking her head.

Ethan framed her face with both hands, tipping her head up, his eyes so full of warmth and love gazing into hers. "Being single's not so bad, but being with your forever love is so much better."

She instantly choked up. Actually hearing "forever love" coming from this tough, formerly hard-to-read man zinged a direct hit to her heart. "Eth, you're going to make me cry."

He scooped her up in a hug that lifted her off the ground. "I'll spend the rest of my life making you happy."

"I make me happy. And you do too. Double the happiness. We are lovey-dovey, aren't we?"

"I love it."

"Me too."

He set her down, his hands resting lightly on her waist before leaning down to her ear, his voice a sexy rumble. "I really want to get you alone. Could we cut out early?"

She slid her hand to the back of his neck and brought him close for a kiss. "Yes. Absolutely. Like right now."

He smirked.

She smirked back.

They turned as one to their friends all gathered by the bar. "Have fun, guys!" Ally called.

"We have an early day tomorrow," Ethan said, guiding her quickly toward the door.

Then they ran out the door, hand in hand, eager to get their hands on each other.

EPILOGUE

Four weeks later, Ethan was enjoying his first Thanksgiving with Ally and her family. They'd be heading to the Campbell house for dessert later. He'd taken Zach's advice to get to know Ally's family, even though he normally avoided other people's families, feeling out of place. But Zach had a deep understanding of courtship and marriage customs and it had worked for him, so Ethan figured, yeah, do it right.

Ally's dad, Brian, was a large stocky man with a booming deep voice, who doted on his four daughters. Ally had three older sisters, two blond, one brunette, all married with kids. He'd met her parents before, but this was the first time he met the rest of her family. Her sisters were much more serious and low-key compared to his love's infectious enthusiasm and vibrancy. Her mom, Susan, was sweet and bubbly like Ally and adored her six grandchildren ranging in age from nine months to twelve. Ally's brothers-in-law were okay too.

The food was delicious and all made by the women. He'd been relegated to the living room to watch the football game with the guys. Ally's dad asked him to take the end seat on the sofa next to his recliner and then spent every commercial break quizzing Ethan on his family, what he did in his spare time, and what sports teams he liked. Ethan had been over for dinner a couple of times before without many questions beyond his work, but it seemed him showing up for Thanksgiving made her dad realize how serious Ethan was about Ally. He must've passed inspection because the minute he said he was a diehard Patriots fan, Brian got up and offered him a beer.

Ally's sisters kept looking at him curiously during dinner at the long dining room table, but he kept quiet for the most part, not wanting to interrupt the family's conversation. The kids had their own table set up in the adjacent living room, except for the baby, who sat in a high chair near her parents. They couldn't see the kids, but as soon as the kids finished their dinner, they sure heard them. Ally's mom went in there and, a few minutes later, the kids got quiet. She returned, reporting they were all watching the movie *Elf*, and then took her seat, addressing him directly.

"Ethan, it's our tradition before dessert to go around the table and say the best thing that happened all year. It reminds us to be thankful. Would you like to begin?"

"Oh, boy. I don't want to intrude." He turned to Ally. "You go ahead first."

Ally smiled and said proudly, "Marrying myself."

Her sisters laughed. Everyone else looked confused. Ally quickly explained the whole concept and the empowerment behind it.

"Then what are you doing with this guy?" her dad said, hitching a thumb toward Ethan, probably for his defense.

Ally smiled. "I had to put myself first, be content with me before I could give myself to someone else."

"What do you mean give yourself?" her dad growled.

Her sisters tittered; their husbands remained quiet, probably in sympathy for Ethan being in the hot seat.

Ethan cleared his throat. Maybe this was the moment he'd been waiting for.

"What do you think I mean?" Ally responded calmly. "I love him. I'm divorcing myself now."

Ethan put a hand on her leg. "No, don't do that. I know how much that sologamy ceremony meant to you. I want you to keep that in spirit." He gazed into her beautiful blue eyes. "Hang onto that, honor yourself. And I'll honor you too."

"Oh, Eth."

"I love you." He spoke his truth no matter the circumstances, even with curious witnesses.

She leaned close, smiling. "I love you too."

He kissed her gently and then stood, taking in the curious expressions on everyone's faces. "The best thing to happen to me all year was having Ally in my life."

"Aww," the women chorused.

"You too!" Ally exclaimed. "I should've said that too. Marrying myself and you. Not marrying you, but having you…I mean, not like that! You know—"

"Still my turn," he told her with a wink. He knew how much she loved him and never doubted his importance in her life. They were sure of each other, both of them full of gratitude for the love they shared. "And just as importantly, the best thing to happen to me this year is what's about to happen right now."

He shifted to the other side of Ally's chair so he'd have room to do it right. Pulling the ring from his pocket, down on one knee, he held the ring up to her.

Her sisters gasped in near unison, exclaiming until their mom hushed them.

"Omigod, Eth," Ally said in a breathy voice. She shifted to face him, her cheeks flushed pink, her eyes huge.

He took her hand. "This engagement ring is an antique. It was my mom's ring from her mother-in-law, so it has a lot of family history. I want you to have it."

Ally squeed and nodded, her eyes filling with tears.

He slid the ring on her finger and held it there. "Will you marry me?"

"Yes!" She grabbed his head and kissed him.

Her family was exclaiming and shifting around, but it all faded in the background. He stood and pulled Ally into his arms, his own eyes burning with tears, his chest filled to bursting with happiness. He loved her so damn much.

Someone put a hand on his back, and he glanced over his shoulder.

"Welcome to the family!" her mom exclaimed, and then it seemed everyone was hugging them and congratulating them all at once.

Her dad even brought out a bottle of champagne. "I've been saving this for a special occasion," he said, handing it over to Ethan. "You do the honors."

"Thanks," Ethan said, taking the bottle. It opened with a pop and her whole family cheered.

Once they were all settled back at the table with the champagne, her dad made a toast. "To Ethan and Ally's future happiness. I can see how happy Ally is and, though we've only known Ethan a short time, I can tell he's a good man and will fit right in with our family. Congratulations, you two." He lifted his glass. "To Ethan and Ally." His voice choked at the end and the big man even leaked a tear.

Ethan quickly looked away to find Ally, her mom, and all of her sisters were quietly crying. Geez, it would be tough to be stoic around this family. They all clinked glasses and drank to that heartfelt toast.

And then Ally's mom encouraged everyone to chime in with the best thing that happened to them all year, and damn if they didn't all say the same thing. Every damn one of them said with a big smile: "Watching Ethan's proposal." By the time the third person said it, Ethan gave up the fight, his own eyes leaking. Ally rubbed his back and leaned her head on his shoulder.

Soon they were all digging into dessert, an assortment of homemade pies—pumpkin, pecan, and mince—with vanilla ice cream and whipped cream. Ethan had nearly finished his second helping of pumpkin pie when Ally's mom surprised him.

"I have a question for Ethan and Ally," she started, innocently enough. "Do you plan on having kids?"

Ethan gulped down his pie and glanced at Ally, her face flushed bright red. "Mom!"

"What?" her mom said, lifting a palm. "It's just a question."

Ally grabbed his hand and held it. "We just got engaged. Don't put pressure on us."

"What pressure?" her mom exclaimed. "No pressure." She looked right at Ethan. "Just curious."

"We haven't even talked about it," Ally said, glancing at him. "Let's move along."

Everyone got quiet.

Ally leaned close and whispered in his ear, "Sorry about that."

He smiled and cradled her jaw, gazing into her eyes. "I don't mind." He wanted kids, but he understood that was a private conversation.

Ally met his eyes, seeming to be searching his expression. "Really?"

He kissed her. "Really."

"See, he doesn't mind," her mom put in.

Ally looked to the ceiling. "Ergh."

"We'll get back to you on that," Ethan told Ally's mom.

Her mom must've read between the lines because she immediately beamed a smile at him, turned to Ally's dad, who nodded once, and then conversation returned to normal.

The ring was a little big for Ally, but she assured him it could easily be sized down. He couldn't wait to share their engagement with his family. Ally happily planned their wedding on the drive over to the Campbell house—something fun but still serious, "a little unconventional" was how she put it. Just like his bride. He readily agreed to anything and everything. Outdoors? Absolutely. Piñata? Why not. Cake buffet? Bring it on. Bride and groom dance with confetti cannons showering them with confetti? Uh, sure. The only thing he cared about was making it official. He didn't bring up the kid conversation, not wanting to rush her since she was younger than him, and also because he wanted her to enjoy this whole engagement moment. But it was definitely on his mind.

The moment he stepped into the Campbell house, he

stood in front of the TV, where all the guys were glued to the football game, and announced, "Ally and I are engaged."

Ally held up her ring hand and beamed.

"Congratulations!" his dad said, and then everyone jumped in, congratulating them, the guys all pounding him on the back.

"Another one bites the dust," Ben quipped.

Ethan bumped him with his shoulder. "You're next, Mr. Wright."

"Never! I'm nobody's Mr. Right."

"That's for sure," Josh said.

Everyone laughed.

He joined his family, taking a seat on an open chair and pulling Ally into his lap, wrapping his arms around her from behind. He whispered in her ear, "You gonna be Mrs. Case or Ms. Bloom?"

She turned and smiled. "I'll be Mrs. Case if you give me a bun in the oven."

His eyes teared up, his throat tight, so glad she was on board. He'd hoped, but he didn't know for sure until now. "I want that so much. I want wild kids that hike and camp and fish—"

"You want mini park rangers. Ha! What if they're girls?"

"Same thing."

"What if they want to play dress up and have tea parties? I did."

He thought about that. "I'll do that too as long as the tea parties happen outdoors."

She laughed and snuggled close. He breathed in the soft flowery scent of the woman he loved with a full open heart, finally one hundred percent content.

Dear Readers,

Will Josh and Clarissa last? Will Hailey plan her heart out and drive everyone crazy? Will they both miss the excitement of their sparring? Stay tuned. Ben Wright might be Missy's Mr. Wrong now, but Fate might have other plans. Next up is Ben and Missy's story, *Resisting Fate*, book 7 in the Happy Endings Book Club series. Join the club and get your happy ending!

Resisting Fate

Is fate playing matchmaker?

Missy Higgins isn't looking for a man, yet everywhere she turns, sexy Ben Wright pops up. A harmless flirtation, nothing more, until Ben wanders into the Christmas craft bazaar just as her horrible ex appears. It's Ben to the rescue as her fake boyfriend with a scorching kiss that leaves her breathless and weak in the knees.

Mind. Blown. (Though she insists it's a onetime thing).

But when Ben shows up just as she's getting fired and offers her a holiday job she desperately needs, she has to wonder if fate might be telling her something. Like screw professional boundaries, give in to uncontrollable lust, and let a man into her heart. How can she resist fate when Ben is irresistible?

Sign up for my newsletter and never miss a new release! kyliegilmore.com/newsletter

ALSO BY KYLIE GILMORE

Unleashed Romance <<steamy romcoms with dogs!

Fetching (Book 1)

Dashing (Book 2)

Sporting (Book 3)

Toying (Book 4)

Blazing (Book 5)

Chasing (Book 6)

Daring (Book 7)

Leading (Book 8)

Racing (Book 9)

Loving (Book 10)

The Clover Park Series <<brothers who put family first!

The Opposite of Wild (Book 1)

Daisy Does It All (Book 2)

Bad Taste in Men (Book 3)

Kissing Santa (Book 4)

Restless Harmony (Book 5)

Not My Romeo (Book 6)

Rev Me Up (Book 7)

An Ambitious Engagement (Book 8)

Clutch Player (Book 9)

A Tempting Friendship (Book 10)

Clover Park Bride: Nico and Lily's Wedding

A Valentine's Day Gift (Book 11)

Maggie Meets Her Match (Book 12)

The Clover Park STUDS series <<hawt geeks who unleash into studs!

Almost Over It (Book 1)

Almost Married (Book 2)

Almost Fate (Book 3)

Almost in Love (Book 4)

Almost Romance (Book 5)

Almost Hitched (Book 6)

Happy Endings Book Club Series <<the Campbell family and a romance book club collide!

Hidden Hollywood (Book 1)

Inviting Trouble (Book 2)

So Revealing (Book 3)

Formal Arrangement (Book 4)

Bad Boy Done Wrong (Book 5)

Mess With Me (Book 6)

Resisting Fate (Book 7)

Chance of Romance (Book 8)

Wicked Flirt (Book 9)

An Inconvenient Plan (Book 10)

A Happy Endings Wedding (Book 11)

The Rourkes Series <<swoonworthy princes and kickass princesses!

Royal Catch (Book 1)

Royal Hottie (Book 2)

Royal Darling (Book 3)

Royal Charmer (Book 4)

Royal Player (Book 5)

Royal Shark (Book 6)

Rogue Prince (Book 7)

Rogue Gentleman (Book 8)

Rogue Rascal (Book 9)

Rogue Angel (Book 10)

Rogue Devil (Book 11)

Rogue Beast (Book 12)

Check out my website for the most up-to-date list of my books:
kyliegilmore.com/books

ABOUT THE AUTHOR

Kylie Gilmore is the *USA Today* bestselling author of the Unleashed Romance series, the Rourkes series, the Happy Endings Book Club series, the Clover Park series, and the Clover Park STUDS series. She writes humorous romance that makes you laugh, cry, and reach for a cold glass of water.

Kylie lives in New York with her family, two cats, and a nutso dog. When she's not writing, reading hot romance, or dutifully taking notes at writing conferences, you can find her flexing her muscles all the way to the high cabinet for her secret chocolate stash.

Sign up for Kylie's Newsletter and get a FREE book! kyliegilmore.com/newsletter

For text alerts on Kylie's new releases, text KYLIE to the number (888) 707-3025. (US only)

For more fun stuff check out Kylie's website https://www.kyliegilmore.com.

Thanks for reading *Mess With Me.* I hope you enjoyed it. Would you like to know about new releases? You can sign up for my new release email list at kyliegilmore.com/newsletter. I promise not to clog your inbox! Only new release info, sales, and some fun giveaways.

I love to hear from readers! You can find me at:
    kyliegilmore.com
    Instagram.com/kyliegilmore
    Facebook.com/KylieGilmoreToo
    Twitter @KylieGilmoreToo

If you liked Ethan and Ally's story, please leave a review on your favorite retailer's website or Goodreads. Thank you.